All rights reserved.
Copyright © 2019 by Anne E.G. Nydam
This book may not be reproduced in whole or in part without permission.
ISBN 978-0-9822766-8-6

Library of Congress Control Number:2019909760

For more information about my work, visit my web site
nydamprints.com

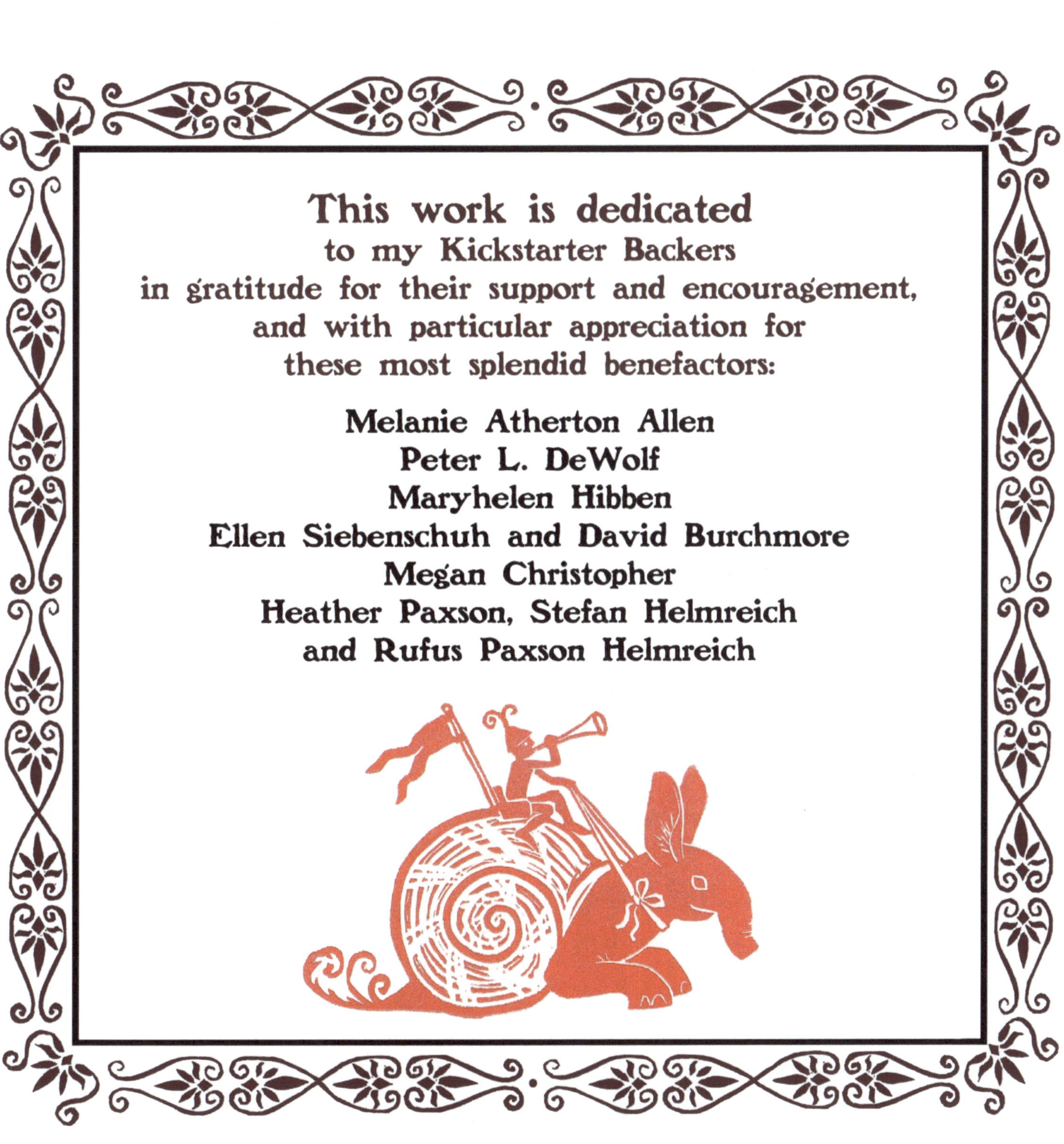

This work is dedicated
to my Kickstarter Backers
in gratitude for their support and encouragement,
and with particular appreciation for
these most splendid benefactors:

Melanie Atherton Allen
Peter L. DeWolf
Maryhelen Hibben
Ellen Siebenschuh and David Burchmore
Megan Christopher
Heather Paxson, Stefan Helmreich
and Rufus Paxson Helmreich

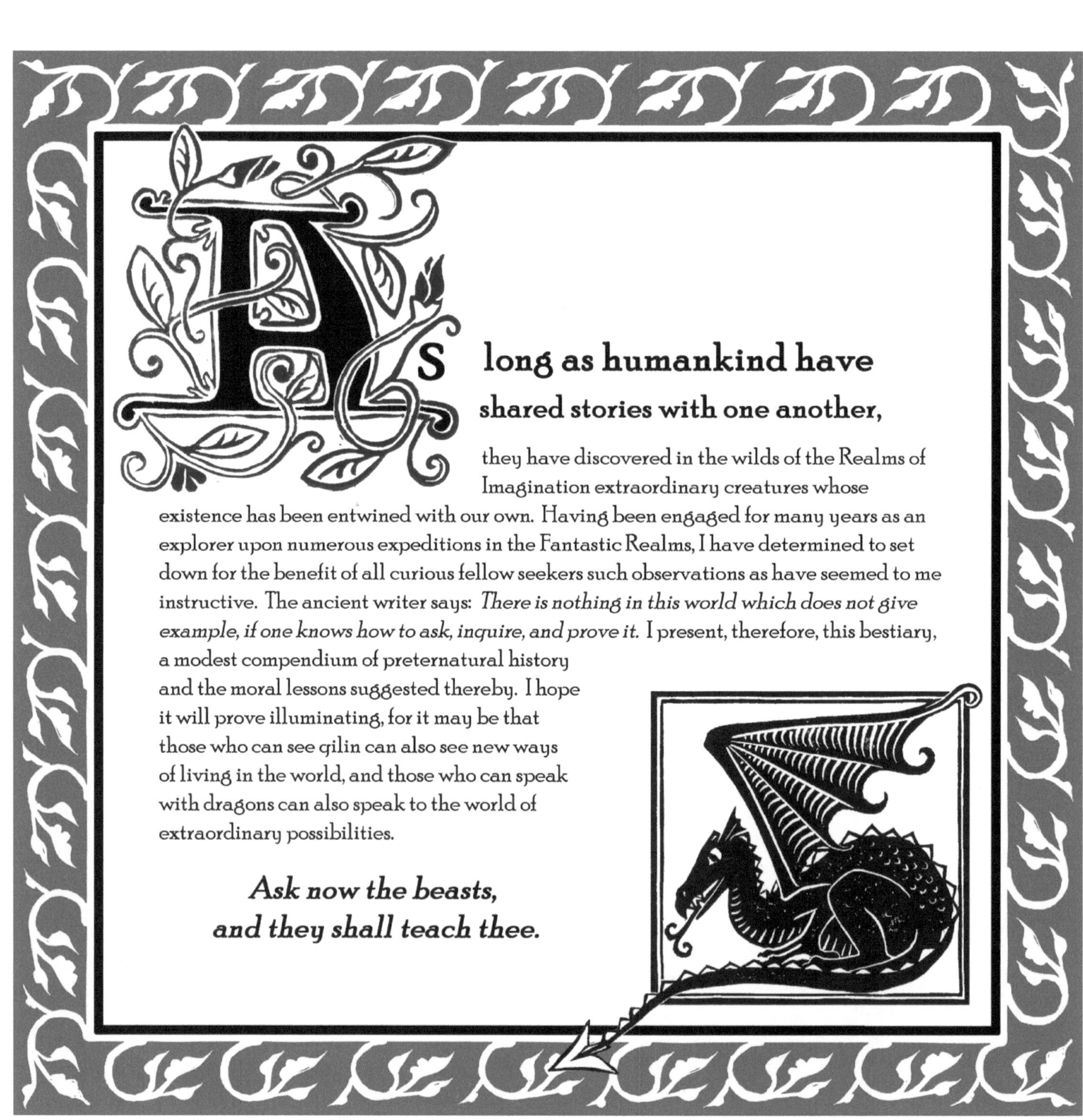

As long as humankind have shared stories with one another,

they have discovered in the wilds of the Realms of Imagination extraordinary creatures whose existence has been entwined with our own. Having been engaged for many years as an explorer upon numerous expeditions in the Fantastic Realms, I have determined to set down for the benefit of all curious fellow seekers such observations as have seemed to me instructive. The ancient writer says: *There is nothing in this world which does not give example, if one knows how to ask, inquire, and prove it.* I present, therefore, this bestiary, a modest compendium of preternatural history and the moral lessons suggested thereby. I hope it will prove illuminating, for it may be that those who can see qilin can also see new ways of living in the world, and those who can speak with dragons can also speak to the world of extraordinary possibilities.

Ask now the beasts,
and they shall teach thee.

Aa

Of the AMPHIPTERE

The amphiptere is a winged serpent. The ancient writer says: *The trees which bear frankincense are guarded by winged serpents, small in size, and of varied colours, a great number round each tree. There is nothing but the smoke of bitter wood that will drive them away from the trees.*

So say ancient writers, describing how merchants of Arabia obtain the highly valued frankincense, for their chief interest is in the use humans may make of the natural world. But what shall *I* say of the amphiptere? For it is the purpose of this work not only to describe the strange and wondrous creatures of the Realms of Imagination, but also to learn from them such lessons as may guide and nourish our own spirits. The amphiptere, then, is a creature about which learned men have little to say except how to eradicate it, and yet is it not marvelous that a creature can be possessed of deadly venom yet also possessed of protecting wings? Like the snake it sheds its skin to be born anew, and like the bird it flies free of earth in image of the soul. Surely there must be more to understand and celebrate in a creature so remarkable.

Let us then say, that from the amphiptere we learn to look at every creature not only as past writers have seen them, not only as men of commerce have judged their value to profit, not only as ignorant men have viewed them with fear. Rather we must wonder at their marvelous qualities and examine what their existence in the world can illuminate about our own. With this perspective we shall be well prepared to study whatever fabulous creatures we encounter.

Of the ASPIDOCHELONE

In the vast and distant oceans of the imagination, curious sailors may be fortunate enough to discover an enormous sea turtle called aspidochelone, of the size of an island, which serves as ground and home to a city of seafaring people. In past centuries sailors were wont to fear the aspidochelone, believing it to be a snare intent upon deceiving them, luring them with the semblance of land only to sink beneath their feet. The ancient writer says: *Seamen imagine they are gazing upon an island, and moor their high-prowed ships with cables fast to the false land. The weary-hearted sailors then encamp, dreaming not of peril. On the island they start a fire, kindle a mounting flame. Now when the cunning plotter, aspidochelone, feels that the seamen are firmly established upon him, and have settled down to enjoy their meal, he sinks without warning into the salt wave with his prey, and makes for the bottom, thus whelming ships and men in that abode of death. Such is the way of demons, the wont of devils: they spend their lives in outwitting men by their secret power.*

But another story is told, that many centuries ago three ships full of desperate people sailed away with their families to escape oppression in their own land, only to encounter a violent storm at sea. Battered and lost, the ships floated with torn sails and broken rudders until the people aboard were nigh to losing all hope. It was then that they saw what they took to be an island and managed to bring their ships to shore. The aspidochelone, for such it was they had encountered, so far from destroying them, took pity on the families and allowed them to build their lives anew in peace upon its back. In return the people of this town protect and feed the aspidochelone, as well as sharing companionship with it, for it is the only one of its kind, of long memory and great wisdom. It carries its town across the seas, wherever it and its people wish to harvest the seagrasses or to trade, and they are at home in all the oceans.

From the aspidochelone and its human partners we learn to be not so hasty to assume malice in the intentions of others, for most beings wish only to live their lives in peace. Fear of that which we do not understand may deprive us of much mutual benefit, while genuine care for the well-being of others brings well-being to us all.

Bb

Of the BAKU

    In the land of Japan far to the east there dwell quiet creatures who are seldom seen, and then only in the shadows. With their sharp tusks and paws like tigers, they may seem dangerous, but they are shy and mild of manner. Their chief food is the nightmares of sleeping humans, and with their elephant-like trunks they snuff and forage through the night in search of bad dreams to eat. The ancient writer says: *It was on a very sultry night, during the Period of Greatest Heat, that I last saw the Baku. I had just awakened out of misery; and the hour was the Hour of the Ox; and the Baku came in through the window to ask, "Have you anything for me to eat?"*

    Some children learn to summon a baku if they should awaken in the darkness with a nightmare, calling out thrice, "*Baku kuraë!* Honorable Baku, come eat my dream!" But a baku must never be called for less than a nightmare, lest it find insufficient nourishment and be forced to eat additional dreams, as well. And what becomes of one whose dreams are all eaten, the good as well as the bad? How can one live without dreams to cherish?

    Likewise, a baku, too, needs dreams of its own to cherish and to teach it how to strive toward all its best possibilities. The baku remind us that those who tend our dreams, who soothe our nightmares and encourage our deepest hopes, must all have dreams of their own. Let us not forget that our parents, teachers, mentors, heroes, sisters, and brothers, as well as the baku themselves, must be given the opportunity and encouragement to live into their own best dreams.

Of the BUNYIP

The bunyip is a creature of the waterholes and billabongs of the land of Australia far to the south. It is known to have a terrifying cry and to be relentless in the protection of its young, but little is known of its appearance, although one ancient writer says: *It has a head resembling an emu, with a long bill, at the extremity of which is a transverse projection on each side, with serrated edges like the bone of the stingray. Its body and legs partake of the nature of the alligator. The hind legs are remarkably thick and strong, and the fore legs are much longer, but still of great strength.*

The bunyip commands not only sharp claws and a crushing grasp, but the ability to make waters rise until its victims are overtaken by the flood. Many are the reports of hunters drowned by rising water after rashly capturing an infant bunyip. It may also be that bunyips participated in the shaping of Australia, forming mountains, waterholes, and other geographical features in their travels across the land in the time when things were created. Thus their hostility toward humans is reserved for those who encroach upon the land and waters the bunyips love.

The bunyip therefore signifies the interconnectedness of the natural world. Just as danger to young bunyips causes disruption to the waters, so all that lives on Earth is entwined with water, forests, soil, and weather. It is wise to remember that damage to any part of nature may cause damage and chaos across all of nature.

C c

Of the
CAPYBUREAU

The capybureau is a placid, gregarious beast, grazing in small flocks in marshy lands, where many laugh to see it, for truly it is quite ridiculous that a creature should have drawers in its side like a piece of furniture. Yet despite their absurd appearance, drawers are not without practical use, for the capybureau carries its young therein, where they can reach the grasses to graze without becoming lost in the deeper waters of the marsh. When danger rises, the capybureaus close their drawers against attack and carry their young safely away. So, too, in the dry season when the pups are old enough to walk on their own and the flock must travel across barren land between water holes, each capybureau can pack a partner's drawers with fresh greens to sustain it on the journey.

The capybureau thus signifies the importance of working together in community, for a capybureau cannot graze from its own drawers, but must carry fodder for another member of the flock. Each beast must help those around it, and be helped by them in turn, lest they all starve. One capybureau alone cannot survive the dry season, but together the flock remains strong.

Of the CHERUFE

There dwell in the heart of the tall and jagged mountains of Chile in the south, creatures roughly human in form, but with scaly skin of stone, and core of fiery magma. Cherufes are known for their fierce and angry nature, and they rattle the very mountains from within, and hurl hot rocks from their molten cores. Their tantrums cause the mountains to smoke and flame, and their discontent shakes the earth. Some people believe that a human must be killed, sacrificed to satisfy the anger of a cherufe, but of course one person's pain cannot relieve another's misery. When a cherufe is angry it is wiser to avoid it, keeping to a safe distance, than to reason or offer bargains. Rage that demands the agony of another can never find itself satisfied.

Although a cherufe cannot be soothed, nevertheless we can learn by considering its state. When you are miserable and uncomfortable, do you not wiggle and squirm like a cherufe in the core of a fiery mountain? When you are irritable, do you not spew smoke and spit fire until you make those around you miserable in equal measure? But if you can calm yourself long enough, you know that making other people suffer cannot relieve your own suffering. You must allow the mountain to contain and steady you until your anger cools or finds release in more constructive purpose.

Of the DRAGON

Dd

I might hold it needless to describe the dragon, most famous of magical reptiles, yet the naturalist must assume nothing, and indeed, there is such variability within dragon-kind that it would be well to avoid confusion. The most typical dragon is long-necked, long-tailed, and with teeth and claws like daggers. Most dragons have leathery wings and four legs, and can spew poison or fire from their throats.

The ancient writer says: *This year dire forewarnings came over the land of the Northumbrians, and miserably terrified the people; these were excessive whirl-winds, and lightnings; and fiery dragons were seen flying in the air. A great famine soon followed these tokens.* In this record the fear that dragons inspire is clear, for the mere sight of a dragon is followed by distress. Another ancient writer makes the dragons' savage proclivities yet clearer, saying: *Their cruel cursed enemy, an huge great Dragon horrible in sight, with murdrous ravine, and devouring might, their kingdome spoild, and countrey wasted quite.*

All people have heard such terrifying tales of dragons, and many ancient accounts tell of dragons devouring villagers and in turn being slain by knights, farmers, and saints. These histories demonstrate that even the cruellest monsters can be defeated. A single hero, sometimes even a hero without a warrior's strength or armor, can challenge great evil and, with courage, creativity, and virtue, bring down the beast. From these tales of dragonslayers we are reminded that we each have the power to stand up against the wrongs we witness. Any one of us can be a hero when need arises, and dragons, however powerful they seem, can be overcome.

Our study of the dragon is not yet complete, however, for there is more to be learned from closer examination of these tales, and we may note that it is always the conquering knight whose tale we tell. Pity it is that so few knights were known to take statements from offending dragons before attacking, but those records that survive demonstrate that most dragons who steal farmer's livestock are simply hungry, as any animal may be. Dragons are much like humans in being creatures of intelligence and free will. For this reason you will find some dragons of deep wisdom and benevolence, and others of wickedness most dreadful. Those dragons who devour livestock may simply be hungry, but those who devour humans do so in the full knowledge that they spread terror. Consider, however, that it is not only dragons who may slaughter people, for knights have also been known to do so. Surely to inflict fear and misery deliberately upon others is the mark of a monster, whether performed by a dragon or by a knight.

Therefore, from the dragon we also learn that though all thinking, speaking creatures are inclined to believe themselves justified in their actions, yet we must all test our own impulses against the light of love within us lest, whatever our outward form, we become monsters.

Ee

Of the EALE

The eale is said to dwell in Æthiopia, and its peculiarity is that its two long horns can be swivelled about on its head to face in whatever directions, together or separately, the eale deems most to its purpose. The ancient writer says: *The Eale is armed with horns above a cubit long, plyable to what use soever he wishes to put them. For they are not stiff, but are bowed as need shall require in fighting: of*

which he putteth out the one when he fighteth, and rolleth up the other. Sometimes the eale may choose to defend itself with both horns, while at other times it may turn its horns away and forbear to attack. Still other times it may strike with one horn while holding the other out of the way, to be used as an alternate should the first horn sustain damage, and at still other times can the eale defend itself from attack from two directions at once.

The eale therefore signifies the value of being circumspect in our responses to threats, keeping multiple options open rather than blindly charging forth in our first impetuous reaction, for it may happen that a precipitous impulse to strike or a rush to act is unwise, or that focussing on a single peril may blind us to a second. It is always advisable to have, as it were, two horns to one's brow.

Of the EMELA-NTOUKA

In the swamps of the Congo in equatorial Africa there dwells an enormous creature, as large as an elephant, but with a tail like a crocodile and a long, sharp horn upon its nose. Although the emela-ntouka is vegetarian in diet, the ancient writers say that its name means *killer of elephants*, for it is so aggressive in defending its territory that it will attack any creature it encounters, slaying even elephants with its horn. No one knows why emela-ntoukas are so belligerent, but it can be observed that in driving away all whom they consider enemies, they drive away equally all who might have been friends. Consider that although the emela-ntouka is stronger than the elephant and destroys the elephant in battle, yet the elephant has its herd, while the emela-ntouka is forever alone.

In the emela-ntouka we observe the lesson that while strength and violence may be effective at gaining power, they are poor indeed at gaining security, for as long as one's power comes from cruelty, one will always feel alone and under constant threat.

Of the FAIRY

    Fairies are a type of sprite, like humans in form, but with delicate wings like those of butterflies or other insects. Furthermore, they are of diminutive stature that can vary from the size of a human child to no larger than a bumblebee. Fairies are seldom visible to humans for they are small and shy, and their lives are with the flowers and leaves and sprouting tendrils of nature. One might conclude from this that they are lowly, insignificant, and without importance, and yet are they not powerfully magical beings? From small glamours to mighty storms, fairies can disorient the wisest man, dizzy the strongest, and bestow otherworldly vision upon the most innocent. The ancient writer says: *Such power there with her presence came*

> *Sterne Tempests she alayd,*
> *The cruell Tiger she could tame,*
> *She raging Torrents stayd.*

    By the fairies we may be reminded that those who live to tend and nurture life are among the most powerful beings there are, far more magical than those who, in their greed for power, ignore or fail to notice the small burgeonings of life, for seeds sprout even in the most barren waste, and stretching roots crack even stone.

Of the FUR-BEARING TROUT

The fur-bearing trout dwells in the coldest rivers, lakes, and mountain streams of North America, where it grows a thick wool fleece to insulate it from the icy water. The people of Minnesota attempt to catch these fish in matching pairs so that they can make the fishfurs into mittens or slippers. The species endemic to Vermont, however, loses its fur instantly upon being taken from the water into the air, much to the chagrin of curious anglers. Anglers are justified in their curiosity, for a wooly fish may indeed seem strange, but what could be more reasonable than a warm coat for protection from the cold?

The fur-bearing trout demonstrates the universal need for that feeling which scholars identify as *the warm fuzzies*, for the world can be cold and everyone benefits from reminders that there is much warmth to be shared. Whether fish or human, whether naturally furred or provided with cozy slippers, we all need those feelings of happiness, contentment, and sentimentality that inspire us to be good to one another.

G g

Of the
GNOME

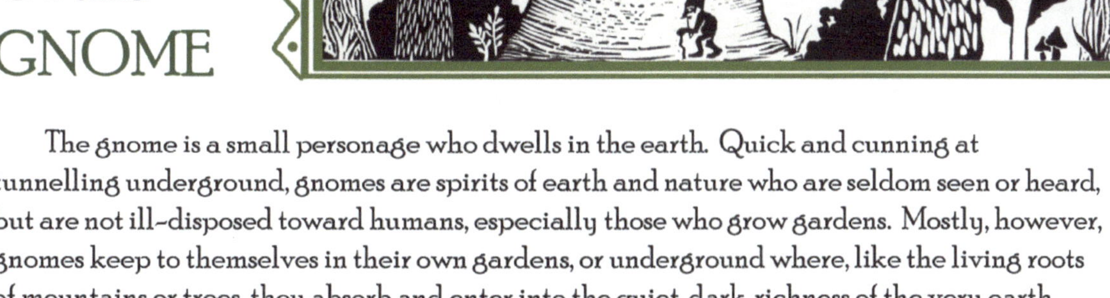

The gnome is a small personage who dwells in the earth. Quick and cunning at tunnelling underground, gnomes are spirits of earth and nature who are seldom seen or heard, but are not ill-disposed toward humans, especially those who grow gardens. Mostly, however, gnomes keep to themselves in their own gardens, or underground where, like the living roots of mountains or trees, they absorb and enter into the quiet, dark, richness of the very earth.

From the gnomes we learn the importance of silence, and replenishing our grounding in nature, for the human world of hustle and bustle and noise rises at times to a floodtide to unmoor us from our souls' peace. If, like the gnomes, we take opportunities to be in silence in the presence of the earth and its growing things, we are restored. We, too, are part of this living earth, and our spirits will always be nurtured thereby. Those who can sit outside and feel leaves or rooted rock beneath them should not neglect to take time to do so. However, even when we cannot find such natural sites we may sometimes take a moment to lay our hands on the bark of a curbside tree, or to grow some small plant in a pot, placing seeds into soil so that, like the gnomes, we may be nourished by the earth.

Of the GRIFFIN

The griffin is a creature of hybrid form, being like a lion in body, but with the head, forelimbs, and wings of an eagle, and sacred to the sun. Moreover, it is larger and stronger than either lion or eagle, able to seize and bear away a horse or ox in its talons, for which reason griffins are well-suited for their role as guardians. The ancient writer says: *So doth it well make out the properties of a Guardian, or any person entrusted; the ears implying attention, the wings celerity of execution, the Lion-like shape, courage and audacity, the hooked bill, reservance and tenacity. It is also an Emblem of valour and magnanimity, as being compounded of the Eagle and Lion, the noblest Animals in their kinds.*

Merchants who have travelled to the wastes of Central Asia where griffins dwell are wont to say that the griffin is most jealous in guarding gold, but know this: it is those very merchants themselves who greed after treasure, journeying to the griffins' home in hope of gathering the profuse gold which occurs in the rocks of which the griffins build their nests. To seize this precious metal, merchants often destroy the nests, ruthlessly slaughtering the eggs and unfledged cubs within. Thus it is solely in order to protect their young from these gold-hunters that griffins are so ferocious.

So it is that the griffin when fully grown is the fiercest guardian of all, yet when young is the thing most fiercely guarded. By this we are reminded that no child is yet what it will become. Those who are weak may yet become strong, those who are slow may yet become swift. Furthermore, we must care for all children as our greatest treasure, far more precious than gold, so that when their time comes, they, too, may grow strong and fly.

Of the HERCINIA

Hh

People have long feared the great, deep forests of the world, dark realms woven of trees and shadows, terrifying unknown beasts, and labyrinthine pathless ways. It is in such forests as these in the north of Europe that hercinias dwell, birds with shimmering feathers that glow brightly in the darkness. Hercinias are not merely beautiful, and one must not value their feathers for mere beauty, because they use their light to guide lost travellers through the forests. Even a single feather fallen from a hercinia continues to glow, still marking the path once the bird itself has flown ahead. The ancient writer says: *The gentle birds called the faire Hercinia, taking the name of that place where they breed, within the night they shine so gloriously, that man's astonied senses they do feed: for in the darke being cast within the way gives light unto the man that goes astray.*

I myself when a traveller was once lost in a dark forest, seeing no way out of the tangle of shadows. I despaired in the night, until I saw what looked like a very star fallen from the heavens to light the way. It was a glittering bird, flying before me from branch to branch and dropping, as it went, feathers along the path. When, thus guided, I finally reached the edge of the wildwood and wept with relief to see the light of dawn spreading across the broad, open hillside that led home, I turned to see the hercinia loose one last feather as a farewell gift, and flit away, a shooting star, back into the depths of the forest to guide another. I have kept that feather always since then, and still it glows softly in the night to remind me of that hope.

The hercinia teaches us that even in times of darkness, we can follow the light. You must not panic or give in to despair, believing that you are alone in the darkness. Neither should you outrun your guide, believing that you know your own way ahead. Rather, have faith that the light can guide you, one step at a time, ever toward the love that is home.

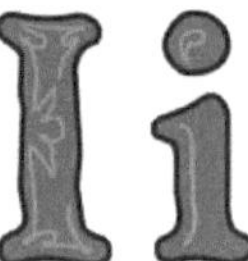

Of the ISNASHI

The isnashi is a large beast covered in long, coarse hair so rank in odor that strong hunters have become dizzy and lost consciousness at the stench of it. Its claws turn backwards on its feet, and it has only one eye, but it has a second mouth, in the center of its chest, from which it roars mightily. It dwells deep in the thick jungles to the south of Earth's equator in Brazil and Bolivia, fearing nothing, only that it dislikes open water.

Some say the isnashi is a vicious monster who slaughters men, while others maintain that it is herbivorous and attacks humans only when they transgress the laws of the forest with needless destruction. In these reports of the isnashi we can see, as in the case of the griffin, that stories may tell us as much about the teller as the subject. Perhaps those who claim that the isnashi is vicious are themselves vicious, and color the creature by their own disposition as much as the truth.

From the isnashi, therefore, we learn to assess the perspectives of every tale-teller we hear, and likewise to be aware of our own attitudes and motivations before we tell tales of others.

Of the JUBJUB BIRD

The Jubjub is a mysterious bird that dwells in the tulgey woods in dismal and desolate valleys of European islands. Most people have been told only to *Beware the Jubjub bird*, but know nothing more about it, nor what specific dangers an encounter with a Jubjub may pose. Thus our frightened fancies endow the mystery with horrors, imagining the most vicious and bloodthirsty nightmare. The ancient writer says: *As to temper the Jubjub's a desperate bird, since it lives in perpetual passion*, and one is indeed wise to beware those of such temperament. Yet if we study all the available descriptions of the creature, it seems rather less fearsome, for the ancient writer says further of the Jubjub: *It knows any friend it has met once before; it never will look at a bribe; and in charity meetings it stands at the door and collects.* Surely this is not the terrifying monster we had, in our ignorance, imagined!

From our study of the Jubjub bird we may be reminded that knowledge, like the light turned on in the dark room, can dispel much fear, and even the greatest horrors can be more valiantly faced when openly and accurately seen. Far better to face the truth, however frightening, than to allow our fancies to be twisted by ignorance.

Kk

Of the KASA-OBAKE

The kasa-obake is a strange spirit dwelling in the mountainous islands of Japan. It is much like a paper umbrella in form, but with a single eye and an enormously long tongue. They hop about on their single leg, and on rainy nights become quite boisterous, sometimes even playing pranks on travellers, such as blowing them into the air. It would seem that some spirit pervades even those most mundane objects that attend our daily lives, such that it is wise to treat them with respect. It has often been observed that a tool well-cared for and properly used will serve well, while an abused tool may betray its master, refusing to perform at its best, and perhaps even harming the hand that wields it. Moreover, after one hundred years an object's spirit may become yet more active, whereupon it can take on life and become a blessing or a curse upon its household, in reflection of how it has been treated. The kasa-obake is one such creature, an umbrella that has become animated with spirit. Tales are told of some kasa-obake that become mischievous, teasing and tormenting those who treated them poorly. However, if left to itself a kasa-obake loves nothing better than to catch the wind and dance in the rain.

By the kasa-obake we may be reminded to respect the objects in our lives, neither wasting them nor misusing them, but always mindful that material given by the earth and labor given by human hands went into their making, for which we must ever be grateful. Rather than carelessly breaking a toy or cavalierly throwing away a gadget in order to purchase a shinier one, consider whether you have used the object well, that you may refrain from wastefulness, and so that the object's animate spirit, should it ever in time acquire one, may have no cause to rebuke you.

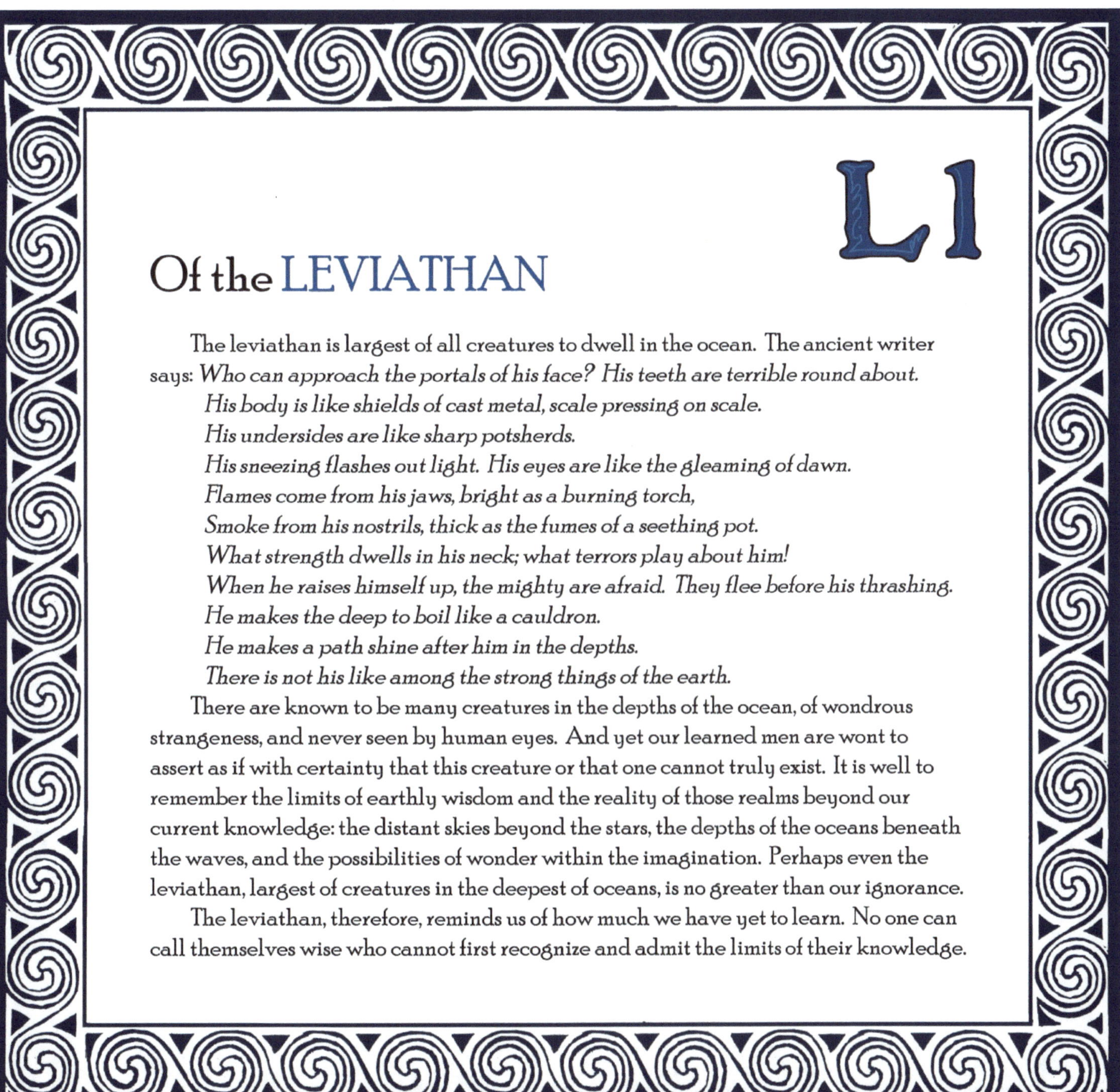

Of the LEVIATHAN

The leviathan is largest of all creatures to dwell in the ocean. The ancient writer says: *Who can approach the portals of his face? His teeth are terrible round about.*

His body is like shields of cast metal, scale pressing on scale.

His undersides are like sharp potsherds.

His sneezing flashes out light. His eyes are like the gleaming of dawn.

Flames come from his jaws, bright as a burning torch,

Smoke from his nostrils, thick as the fumes of a seething pot.

What strength dwells in his neck; what terrors play about him!

When he raises himself up, the mighty are afraid. They flee before his thrashing.

He makes the deep to boil like a cauldron.

He makes a path shine after him in the depths.

There is not his like among the strong things of the earth.

There are known to be many creatures in the depths of the ocean, of wondrous strangeness, and never seen by human eyes. And yet our learned men are wont to assert as if with certainty that this creature or that one cannot truly exist. It is well to remember the limits of earthly wisdom and the reality of those realms beyond our current knowledge: the distant skies beyond the stars, the depths of the oceans beneath the waves, and the possibilities of wonder within the imagination. Perhaps even the leviathan, largest of creatures in the deepest of oceans, is no greater than our ignorance.

The leviathan, therefore, reminds us of how much we have yet to learn. No one can call themselves wise who cannot first recognize and admit the limits of their knowledge.

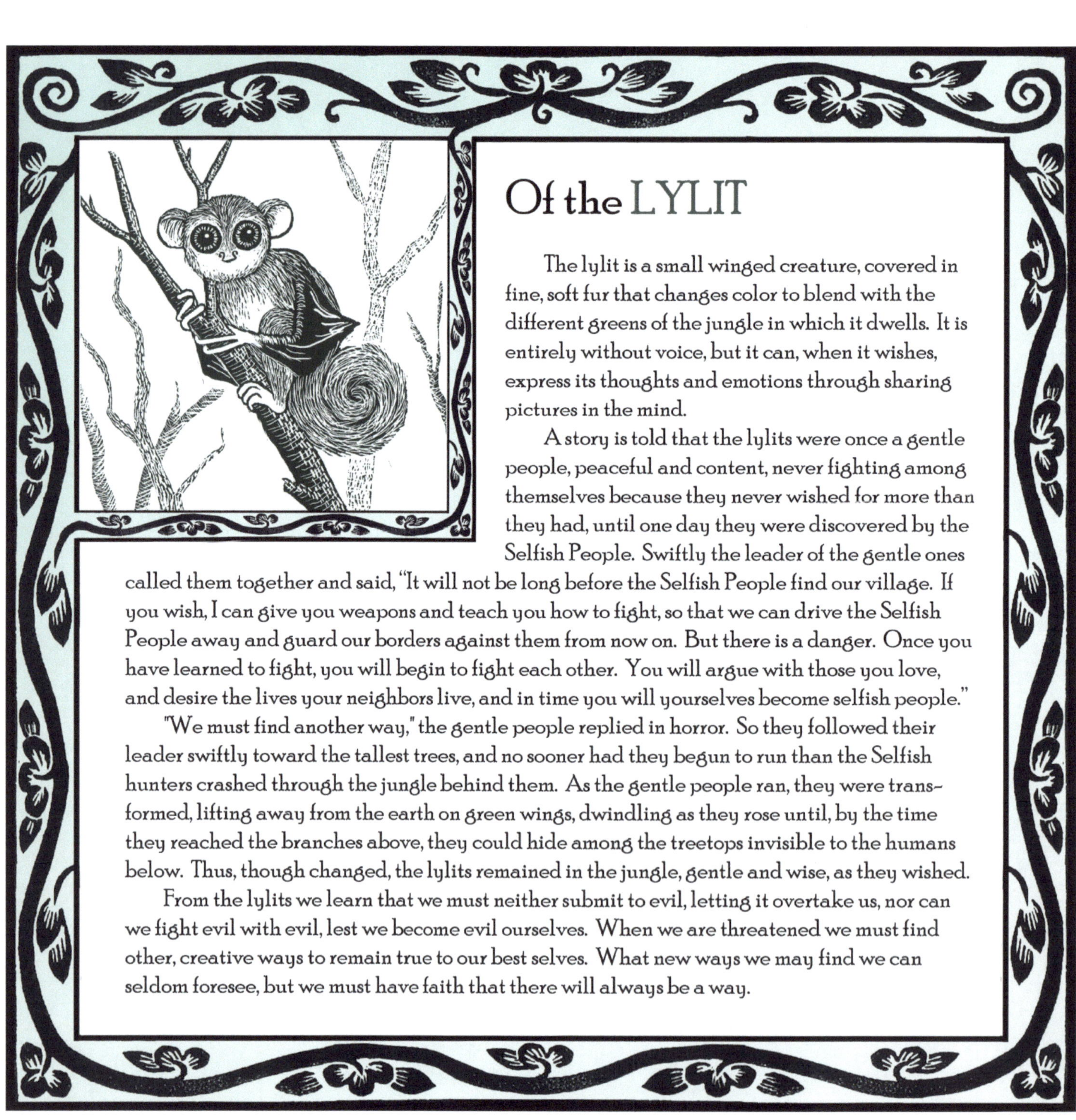

Of the LYLIT

The lylit is a small winged creature, covered in fine, soft fur that changes color to blend with the different greens of the jungle in which it dwells. It is entirely without voice, but it can, when it wishes, express its thoughts and emotions through sharing pictures in the mind.

A story is told that the lylits were once a gentle people, peaceful and content, never fighting among themselves because they never wished for more than they had, until one day they were discovered by the Selfish People. Swiftly the leader of the gentle ones called them together and said, "It will not be long before the Selfish People find our village. If you wish, I can give you weapons and teach you how to fight, so that we can drive the Selfish People away and guard our borders against them from now on. But there is a danger. Once you have learned to fight, you will begin to fight each other. You will argue with those you love, and desire the lives your neighbors live, and in time you will yourselves become selfish people."

"We must find another way," the gentle people replied in horror. So they followed their leader swiftly toward the tallest trees, and no sooner had they begun to run than the Selfish hunters crashed through the jungle behind them. As the gentle people ran, they were transformed, lifting away from the earth on green wings, dwindling as they rose until, by the time they reached the branches above, they could hide among the treetops invisible to the humans below. Thus, though changed, the lylits remained in the jungle, gentle and wise, as they wished.

From the lylits we learn that we must neither submit to evil, letting it overtake us, nor can we fight evil with evil, lest we become evil ourselves. When we are threatened we must find other, creative ways to remain true to our best selves. What new ways we may find we can seldom foresee, but we must have faith that there will always be a way.

M m

Of the
MALACOMORPH

The malacomorph is a mysterious creature with the spiralled shell of a snail. Other than its shell, however, a malacomorph may resemble any sort of creature imaginable, and thus hundreds of unique malacomorphs dwell in the margins of the imagination. The ancient writers say nothing whatsoever about the malacomorph, for although these whimsical creatures appear with remarkable frequency in the illuminations of ancient books, they are never mentioned in these texts, and nor have any of the ancient naturalists examined them. I suspect that they are seldom even noticed by the learned men who study these texts.

The malacomorph teaches us to be observant of all those shy details in the world around us: creatures under leaves and rocks, beauty in forgotten corners, changing expressions in the faces beside us, fleeting glories of light and color; and likewise to be aware of all the small flittings of the imagination, which may lead us to undiscovered treasures. For when we are too busy or too self-important to practice this observation, we deprive ourselves of much wisdom and delight.

Of the MUŠḪUŠŠU

Certain monsters are set as guardians at the gates of a great and ancient city of Mesopotamia, standing stiffly at attention for millennia. They are scaled as dragons, but with hind legs and talons as of eagles, forelegs and paws as of lions, and horns both straight and curved upon their heads. Travellers who enter the gates are awed by the solemnity of these strange and regal beasts, symbols and enforcers of their kingdom's mighty power. However, I have heard an old woman tell that once upon a time, long ago when she was a young child travelling to the great city with her father, she saw from the corner of her eye as they entered through the awesome blue-glazed gate, that one mušḫuššu twitched the tip of its tail. Curious, the girl returned to the gate just before dawn the next morning and witnessed four of the mighty, magical mušḫuššus scampering up from the riverbank, shaking the water droplets in shimmering arcs from their scaly hides as they playfully chased one another back to their posts at the gate. There, in an instant, they became stiff and solemn, guarding their kingdom once again.

Travellers entering the great city who glance at the mušḫuššus only in passing will have little idea what manner of beast they truly are, and few indeed are those people privileged to glimpse the mušḫuššus frolicking among the rushes by the great Euphrates River. Because theirs is a solemn task, they are treated as solemn creatures, but in truth mušḫuššus are playful beasts, as joyous as puppies.

It is wise to remember that even those who perform services for us have lives of their own beyond their work, and that no one can stand at attention or labor perpetually without respite. Even the most invisible or disciplined of workers are more than their work, and even the most responsible and serious of elders must sometimes laugh and play.

DANGER

Of the NINKI NANKA

The Ninki Nanka is a fearsome monster dwelling in the swamps and rivers of western Africa, especially the Gambia and Senegal. Although it is seldom seen, its presence is known, and children are warned never to enter the swamps alone lest the Ninki Nanka devour them. Imagine how easily even a huge beast can lurk in the muddy pools among the roots and weeds, watching and waiting for unwary prey. A swirl of movement in the humid, heavy air, a swish of the turbid water, and suddenly the scaly neck rears up, the horns slash, the powerful teeth clamp on flesh, and another victim disappears beneath the churning water. Surely no one should enter the swamp without being warned of the Ninki Nanka.

The world is full of dangers and every child must learn to face them. Some risks are necessary and help us stretch our abilities and strive toward our dreams, but other risks are foolish and unhealthy, leading us to excessive and purposeless danger. Everyone must learn to discern between the two, and the Ninki Nanka therefore signifies the hope that all parents have for their growing children: *Don't do anything stupid.*

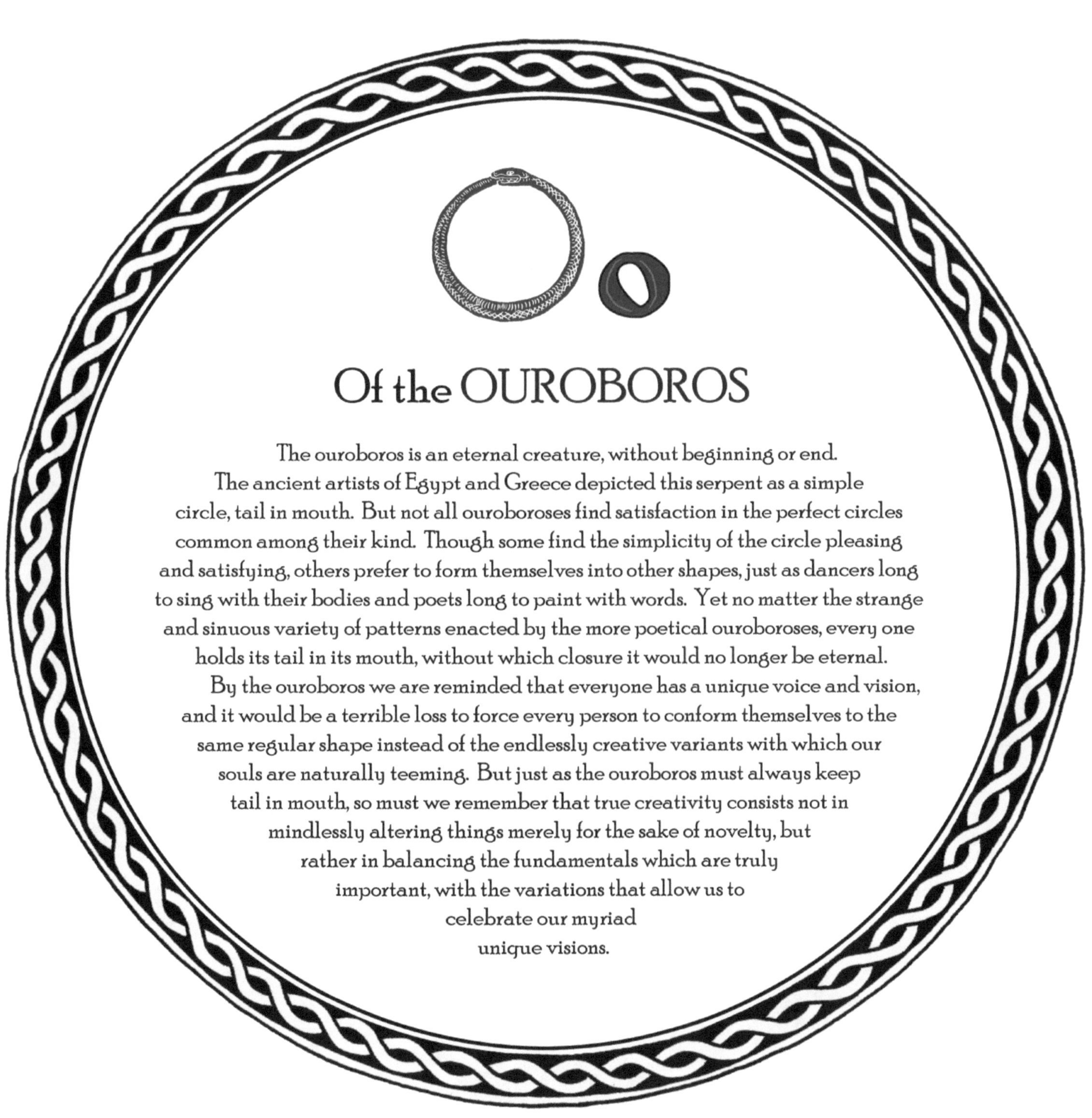

Of the OUROBOROS

The ouroboros is an eternal creature, without beginning or end.
The ancient artists of Egypt and Greece depicted this serpent as a simple
circle, tail in mouth. But not all ouroboroses find satisfaction in the perfect circles
common among their kind. Though some find the simplicity of the circle pleasing
and satisfying, others prefer to form themselves into other shapes, just as dancers long
to sing with their bodies and poets long to paint with words. Yet no matter the strange
and sinuous variety of patterns enacted by the more poetical ouroboroses, every one
holds its tail in its mouth, without which closure it would no longer be eternal.
By the ouroboros we are reminded that everyone has a unique voice and vision,
and it would be a terrible loss to force every person to conform themselves to the
same regular shape instead of the endlessly creative variants with which our
souls are naturally teeming. But just as the ouroboros must always keep
tail in mouth, so must we remember that true creativity consists not in
mindlessly altering things merely for the sake of novelty, but
rather in balancing the fundamentals which are truly
important, with the variations that allow us to
celebrate our myriad
unique visions.

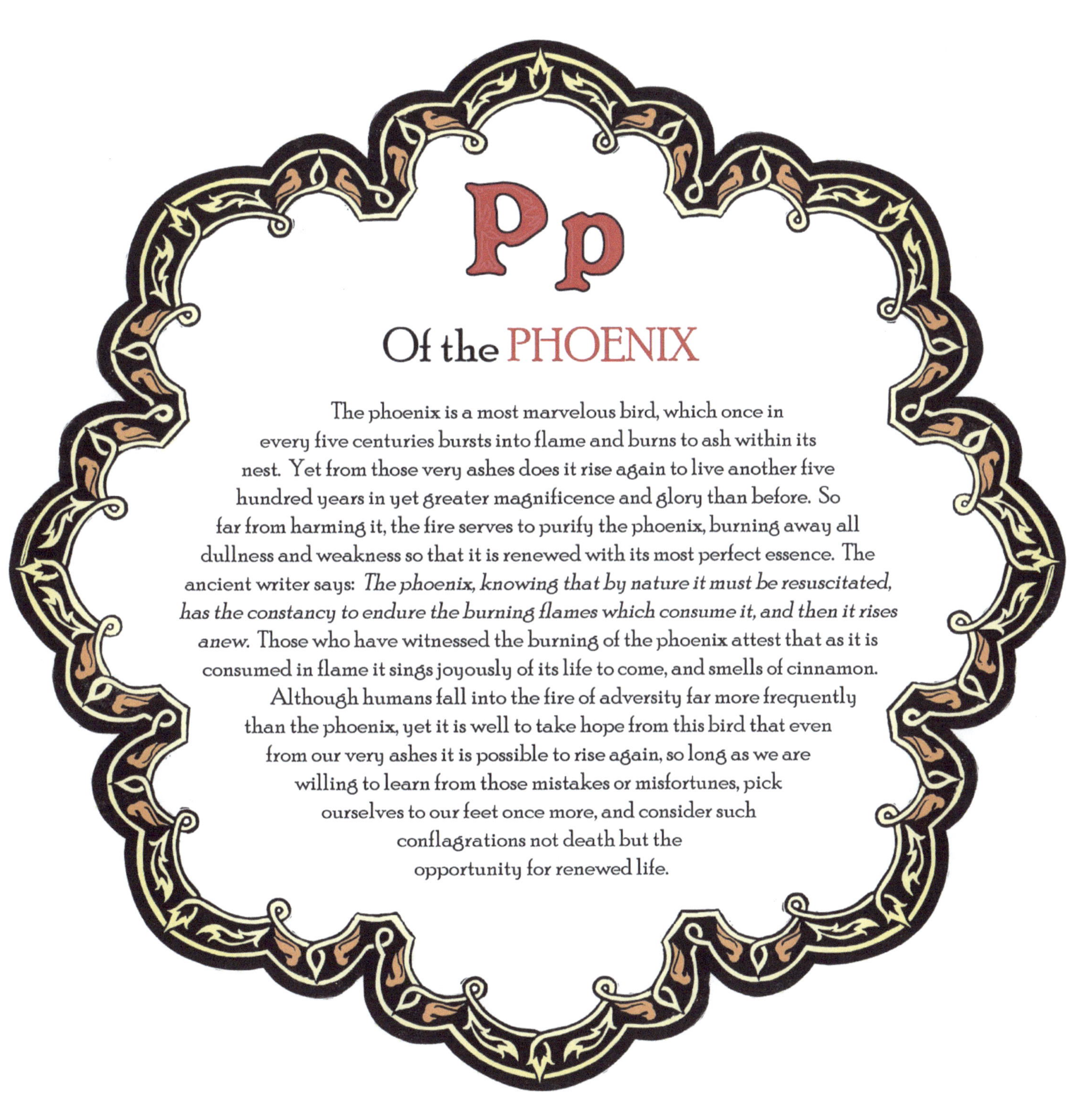

P p

Of the PHOENIX

The phoenix is a most marvelous bird, which once in
every five centuries bursts into flame and burns to ash within its
nest. Yet from those very ashes does it rise again to live another five
hundred years in yet greater magnificence and glory than before. So
far from harming it, the fire serves to purify the phoenix, burning away all
dullness and weakness so that it is renewed with its most perfect essence. The
ancient writer says: *The phoenix, knowing that by nature it must be resuscitated,
has the constancy to endure the burning flames which consume it, and then it rises
anew.* Those who have witnessed the burning of the phoenix attest that as it is
consumed in flame it sings joyously of its life to come, and smells of cinnamon.
Although humans fall into the fire of adversity far more frequently
than the phoenix, yet it is well to take hope from this bird that even
from our very ashes it is possible to rise again, so long as we are
willing to learn from those mistakes or misfortunes, pick
ourselves to our feet once more, and consider such
conflagrations not death but the
opportunity for renewed life.

Of the PTERIPPUS

The pterippus is a winged horse, strong and beautiful in flight. No one fortunate enough to watch a pterippus racing the wind can fail to see the joy with which its hooves dance among the clouds and its wings embrace the sky. The ancient writer says:

As sweeps the whirlwind, heavenward springs
The unfurl'd glory of his wings,
Before the eye can track the flight,
Lost in the azure fields of light.

To witness a pterippus in flight is to see the pure exultation of practicing a gift, for who does not rejoice to perfect a skill that gives such delight?

From the pterippus we can learn to name the things which feed our souls, and practice them. Do not let your gifts languish while pursuing what the world deems of importance, nor ignore those true treasures while gathering up the cold hoard of outward wealth or acclaim; rather cherish those things that give you genuine joy, and do not be shy in sharing them with the world, which hungers for them, though it may not always recognize or acknowledge its own need.

Of the QILIN

The qilin is a most auspicious creature in the land of China, where it dwells. It is covered in brilliant scales and has a mane and tail that flow always upwards like flame. With its slender legs and delicate hooves it is careful to step lightly so that it never harms a living thing, neither crawling insect nor blade of grass. The ancient writer says: *There lives a creature of so gentle kind a nature, on no living thing will tread, no, not e'en the grass in spring; and the horn which crowns its head never injures mortal thing.*

There are those who may say kind words when people are listening, but speak cruelly behind others' backs, or who do what is right only when others are watching, in hope of reward or in pursuit of reputation. The qilin, however, is gentle wherever it walks, and is no less careful of a lowly beetle in the grass than of an emperor. The qilin's perfect integrity gives it the power to stand up to wickedness, for it knows what is right and how to live in peace and honesty with all.

The qilin, therefore, teaches us that integrity gives us strength. We must strive to be true to our own best spirit even when no one else is witness to our deeds, for only in this honesty can we practice the fortitude to do what is right when doing right is not easy.

Nycteris & Flederer's Patent Mechanical Chiropterid (Model 3)

Of the ROBOT

A robot is a creature built by human hands, and can thus be designed in myriad forms. Some of the creations of humans are mere tools, devised by mechanics to perform a task without thought or reflection, and these are common in the mundane world, especially in factories. Other robots, however, are complex creatures capable of life-like action of their own, beings proper that may consider their own place in the universe. Indeed, there is much debate over the essence of a robot, and whether a robot with self-consciousness and will can indeed be said to be alive and have a soul despite its artificial birth. The ancient robot says: *I am fit-ted with Smith & Tin-ker's Improved Com-bi-na-tion Steel Brains. You have no i-de-a how full of ma-chin-er-y I am. I am on-ly a ma-chine. But I can think and speak and act, when I am pro-per-ly wound up.*

One must be clever indeed to build such a complex robot, but cleverness may often fail in wisdom, and thoughtless people seek always for servants who will obey without question, and children who will remain in the mold their parents have created. Some humans are wont to forget that we are not to control the souls of others.

The robot, therefore, signifies the human desire to create things over which we can hold dominance, and the question of when the things we think we control become their own and not ours.

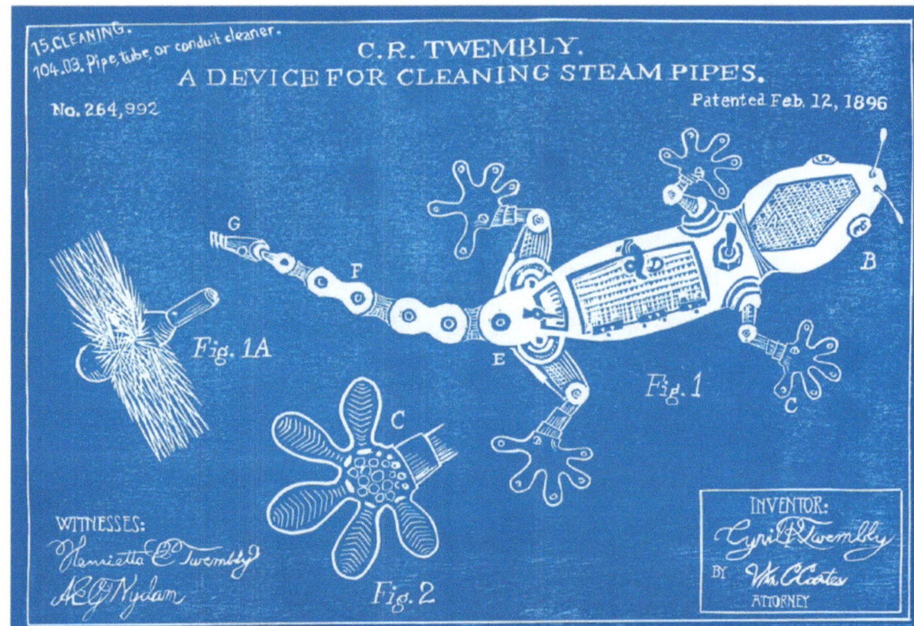

S s

Of the SALAMANDER

Salamanders, as scholars know, are of two sorts. The first are amphibians, born of their own kind as are all earthly creatures. These are very gentle, tender animals that do no harm yet are themselves easily harmed. They are creatures of cool dampness. But the other salamander is an elemental spirit born of fire, wild and unquenchable. It is similar in appearance to the amphibian, but wreathed about in flame. It is said that the fiery salamander must itself be cold in order to survive amid such heat, where it is continually refreshed, receiving all its sustenance from the fire. Moreover, its skin and blood can be used by humans to protect themselves from burning. The ancient writer says: *The fabled Salamander has lived and flourished amid the flames, and has seemed to feed upon the flames that threatened to devour her.*

Both types of salamanders, the earthly and the elemental, are rich jewels in the experience of humans, for were either to disappear from human knowledge, we would be the poorer, and yet both are endangered by too thoughtless a focus on those things deemed of material importance. Thus from the salamander we must learn to value and protect the full variety of marvels present in our world: the remarkable, miraculous creations both of the natural world and of human cultures. For anything once obliterated is impossible to regain, and we have responsibility to consider not only our own short-term desires, but the well-being and richness of generations into the future.

Of the SPACE CREATURE

The story illustrated here for your consideration is of a struthioform astronaut from the far-distant planet Pelavium upon its first discovery of life forms on a moon of Nemelun, with which Pelavium shares a star. Among these newly encountered species are a tentacled crater-dweller, a grove of sentient trees or vines, and the aviansect that dwells thereon, while a cautious frondbrow looks on shyly. All these space creatures are new discoveries to the struthioform, but it should be noted that the struthioform is equally new to them. For they, no more than the denizens of Earth, can never hope to compass the limitless possibilities of life on other worlds. While explorers of the Realms of Imagination have sent expeditions into the far reaches of space to investigate what life may inhabit the worlds beyond our own Earth, we have only begun to plumb these possibilities. The ancient writer says: *Each of the worlds is inhabited by a race essentially different. There are creatures of all possible forms, of all dimensions, of all weights, of all colours, of all sensations, of every variety of characteristics. The universe is infinite. An inexhaustible diversity enriches this marvellous field.* The only thing that is certain is that extra-terrestrial creatures are as intent upon their own purposes as we are upon ours. To the creatures of other planets, we are the space creatures.

By the space creatures, therefore, we are reminded that every being is the center of its own universe, and every creature is to some degree alien to all others. It is wise to remember that our own centrality is only a matter of perspective, so that we may practice patience and understanding when others fail to perceive our untold thoughts or to value our desires as highly as their own.

Plate XXIV: Time Flies
Order Tempusfugita
1
2
3
4
5
6
7
8
9
10
11
12
AGN

Of the TIME FLY

Time flies are an order of insect that comes in many varieties. The ancient writer says: *What faint ticking of ratchets and cogs, what whirring of flywheels and wings I heard, nay felt, as my eyes gradually adjusted to the dim and dusty light in which I found myself. All around me in the gloom I perceived the precise, dry fluttering of the time flies, marking out the seconds and fractions of seconds with the staccato hum of their mysterious horologic rounds. Time itself seemed to whirr past me with the rush of sand through an hourglass, grain by grain, yet fluid as the river.* It is thought that time flies breed in the dust of long-abandoned bell-towers, where the fluttering and buzzing of their wings causes slight vibrations in the flow of time around them. It has been noticed by philosophers that similar vibrations in the flow of time can occur to people engaged in certain activities. That is to say that during the most engrossing of tasks in which we are utterly absorbed, it sometimes happens that time seems to run the faster past us. I myself have found that while I am engaged in my own favorite task of studying, writing, and depicting the Realms of Imagination, several hours may pass over me in a space that seems much shorter. Naturalists may be led to wonder whether such temporal anomalies indicate the presence of a time fly nearby.

It is certain that further study of the time flies will reveal ever more fascinating facets of their life cycle and other attributes, to which end the curious seek out these insects. Should you wish to join the naturalists in their observations, you will find time flies when you're having fun.

Of the TROLL

Trolls are large, strong beings of roughly human form, but without human conscience. They are ill-intentioned and dangerous, but dwell in Europe far to the north, in mountains and deep forests remote from human habitation, and thus they can usually be avoided. When they are encountered, they are far too strong to best in battle, but can often be outwitted.

Many have heard the tale of the troll who lurked beneath a bridge with the intent of catching and devouring those desperate beings who crossed the span in hope of better life on the other side. The ancient writer says:

"Who's that tripping over my bridge?" roared the troll.

"Oh, it is only I, the tiniest billy-goat Gruff," said the billy-goat, with such a small voice.

"Then I'm coming to gobble you up," said the troll.

"Oh no, pray don't take me. I'm too little," said the small billy-goat, "Wait a bit 'til the second billy-goat Gruff comes. He's much bigger."

Thus it is told that in his greed to catch the biggest possible prey, the troll let smaller travellers slip past… until the largest of all turned out to be more than the troll could capture, and he was thus defeated.

There is much to admonish in the behavior of the troll, for although no creature can be blamed for hunger, it is the mark of a troll that he refuses to be satisfied with a sufficiency, and craves always for more than he can possibly use. Should you encounter a troll, you may remember to your advantage that it is his greed that can become his downfall – but remember also the story of the troll should you find yourself becoming greedy for more than you need, for greed makes humans, too, as stupid and cruel as trolls.

U u

Of the UMBRELLAPHANT

The umbrellaphant is a beast native to the rainy regions of the world, and there are three species, the tusk~umbelled, the trunk~umbelled, and the auricle~umbelled, depending upon where the broad parasols of their umbels grow. All three species use their umbels not only to protect their heads from excessive rain or sun, but also to slow their descent when they leap from high places. Truly it is a marvelous sight to witness a herd of umbrellaphants floating from a mountaintop, appearing as light as dandelion down, until they reach the bottom and the ground shakes with their impact, and the puddles splash in fountains beneath their massive feet.

Not only for themselves do the umbrellaphants extend their umbels, however, for they are most welcoming beasts. Should another creature desire refuge, the umbrellaphant will gladly make room, so that it is not uncommon to see a number of smaller birds and beasts accompanying an umbrellaphant, pleased to find shade from the searing sun or shelter from the pelting rain. The ancient writer says: *When caught by a shower, forgetting all fears, they stand underneath the Umbrellaphant's ears.*

From the umbrellaphant we can learn the importance of welcome, and of making others feel accepted. Perhaps it is most especially important to welcome those who are not just like ourselves, for an umbrellaphant's shelter is of far greater importance to creatures who have no umbels of their own, and a kind and welcoming word is of most importance to the stranger.

Of the UNICORN

The unicorn is among the best-known of magical creatures that dwell in the woodlands of Europe, a beautiful beast, in form something like a goat or slender horse, white as mist, and with a single long horn upon its forehead. The ancient writers describe the terrifying fierceness of the unicorn, wildest of beasts, hardest to capture with the weapons of the hunt. Yet when approached in tenderness by an innocent child, the unicorn becomes mild and lies down with the child in gentle amity. The ancient writer says: *The unicorn forgets its ferocity and wildness; and laying aside all fear it will go up to a seated damsel and go to sleep in her lap.* This is well known and presented as a great marvel, but is it not equally true of humankind? A man threatened with weapons and violence becomes violent in return, answering blow for blow until assailant and defender are both grievously wounded. Yet this same man may be brought to gentleness by goodwill, glad to lay down his own weapons to befriend the one who comes without violence.

In the unicorn we see that our actions can be reflected in the actions of those we meet: cruelty with cruelty, anger with anger, and likewise kindness with kindness and love with love. Thus kindness can often conquer where violence fails.

Of the VEGETABLE LAMB

The vegetable lamb appears like any lamb or small sheep, with four hoofed legs and a thick, wooly coat. However, it is not a beast but a plant which is rooted in the ground, where it grows in central Asia. The seed thereof looks like a melon seed, and upon the plant grows a sort of melon or pod, wherein the lamb develops. When the pod opens, the lamb remains attached to its plant by a stem growing from its belly, so that it can graze only to the distance which its stem allows. The ancient writer says: *The plant grows to the height of about three feet, having in lieu of horns two curly locks of hair. If wounded it bleeds; wolves are greedily fond of it; if well grown round with juicy herbage the plant thrives like a lamb in fair pastures; if the grass be cleared away it pines and dies.* There are some wise herbalists who grow their vegetable lambs in pots atop small wheels so that they may easily be rolled to fresh pasturage before consuming all the forage within their reach, for if they were required to remain ever close to their own plot, would they not famish and wither away?

From the vegetable lamb we may learn that every creature needs space to grow and freedom to roam. Even children and those creatures who require our care and protection will surely starve, body and mind, without some ability to stretch themselves and explore their world.

Of the WAPALOOSIE

In the damp forests of northwestern regions of the United States of America dwells a creature peculiarly adapted to climbing trees to reach the shelf or bracket fungus upon which it dines. The wapaloosie is the size of a river otter, but rather more extreme in conformation, moving and climbing as it does in the manner of an inchworm. Its climbing skills are further enhanced by its zygodactyl feet, having two toes pointing forward and two back like a woodpecker, as well as by its spike-tipped tail with which it can anchor itself to a tree. The ancient writer says: *He is able to get the fungus conks with ease, no matter if they are growing on the tip top of a hundred-foot tree. It is a pleasure for one of these animals to climb.* The sight of a wapaloosie humping itself nimbly up and down and from tree to tree is a charming one, and their consumption of the fungus aids greatly in the healthy ecosystem of the forests.

A yet more remarkable feature of the wapaloosie was discovered, however, by a lumberjack who thought to make himself a pair of mittens from a wapaloosie's rich, velvety coat. To the lumberjack's dismay, the mittens never lost their former inhabitant's predilection for climbing, and invariably worked their agile way up his axe handle, and anything else he attempted to grasp. When he laid the mittens down, they immediately began to climb the nearest tree, and were soon lost in the upper branches.

The wapaloosie serves as an example and reminder of the importance of persistence in striving ever upward toward our goals. Like these spry and pertinacious little creatures, we must endeavor to adapt all our habits to further us in our best intentions. This is the true simplicity: to hold fast to our noblest priorities without distraction, for when we have thus aligned our lives with wisdom and virtue, and are so unflagging in our work, then we will come to be as cheerful and steadfast as the wapaloosie, and serve as examples and reminders, in our turn, to others.

EEDOM

Of the WYVERN

The wyvern is of dragon-kind, winged but with two legs only, and generally somewhat smaller than the great dragon. Wyverns are known to rampage at times, devouring livestock and poisoning the air with pestilence. The ancient writer says: *Its glowing greenish eyes had keen and penetrating sight, for often, when flying high in mid-air, the wyvern would swoop suddenly upon some unprotected sheepfold, or traveller wandering in the darkness, and a startled scream, only too quickly smothered, would tell of another victim.*

The wyvern dwells primarily in Europe, and is frequently employed in heraldry, where it poses fiercely on coats of arms. There it is thought to bring fortune in conflict to those who bear its symbol, but what of the wyvern's own fortune? Though wyverns have rampaged over the countryside and posed on coats of arms for centuries, it is not inevitable that they do so always and forever. I myself in my travels once encountered on a rocky tor a restless wyvern who had left his shield to seek his own fortune, hoping to discover what new prospects the world might hold for him.

This wyvern teaches us the power of envisioning new possibilities, for it is easy to assume that the way things are is the only possible way for them to be, and difficult to break free of the assumption that the world cannot be changed or improved. Let us be reminded by the adventuresome wyvern that we need not remain enslaved to things as they are, for the way things are is not inevitable, and we can, with imagination, seek for freedom in new ways of seeing and living in the world.

Of the XANA

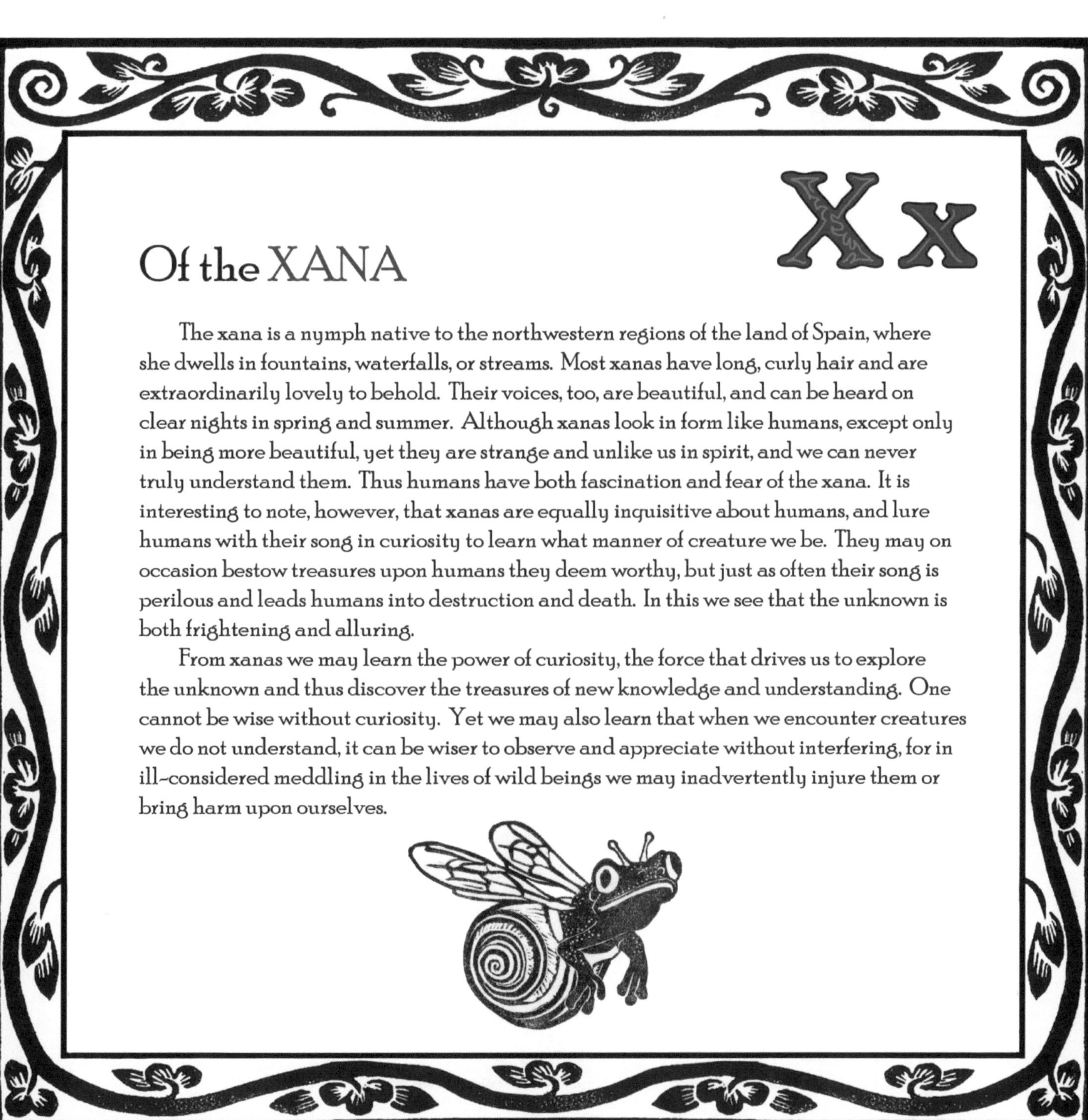

The xana is a nymph native to the northwestern regions of the land of Spain, where she dwells in fountains, waterfalls, or streams. Most xanas have long, curly hair and are extraordinarily lovely to behold. Their voices, too, are beautiful, and can be heard on clear nights in spring and summer. Although xanas look in form like humans, except only in being more beautiful, yet they are strange and unlike us in spirit, and we can never truly understand them. Thus humans have both fascination and fear of the xana. It is interesting to note, however, that xanas are equally inquisitive about humans, and lure humans with their song in curiosity to learn what manner of creature we be. They may on occasion bestow treasures upon humans they deem worthy, but just as often their song is perilous and leads humans into destruction and death. In this we see that the unknown is both frightening and alluring.

From xanas we may learn the power of curiosity, the force that drives us to explore the unknown and thus discover the treasures of new knowledge and understanding. One cannot be wise without curiosity. Yet we may also learn that when we encounter creatures we do not understand, it can be wiser to observe and appreciate without interfering, for in ill-considered meddling in the lives of wild beings we may inadvertently injure them or bring harm upon ourselves.

Of the YALI

    The yali is among the most ferocious of all beasts, fiercer than the lion, stronger than the elephant, and deadlier than the tiger. They are, indeed, as ferocious and terrifying as the untameable forces of nature, and yet these savage monsters are to be found protecting temples far to the south in the land of India, guiding the faithful to those sacred spaces. Is it not remarkable that a beast so monstrous should turn its strength to such reverent purposes?

    The yali thus signifies redemption, for if even beings embodying such violence and fury can choose to use their gifts for good, surely it is not impossible for a human to turn aside from wickedness and try a better path. All creatures have their gifts, and of what sort soever our strengths or talents may be, we can choose to use them in the service of others and all that is good, as the yalis strive to do. It is never too late to choose the path of virtue, nor indeed to choose it again and again, however often we may fall short of our noblest hopes.

Of the YPOTRYLL

The ypotryll is a truly ridiculous beast, appearing to be composed of what random features were pulled from the hat of a careless creator, and let loose into the Realms of Imagination without any particular skills or properties beyond its ungainly appearance. Even its name is a ridiculous-looking word. The ancient writers recount no tales of the ypotryll, no doubt finding it too silly to be worthy of their consideration. It would be easy to scoff at the ypotryll, dismiss it as useless, and sneer at its foolish features, but if we look more closely, we may notice that the ypotryll itself seems perfectly pleased to be here. It cares naught for the scorn of the world, neither allowing itself to be saddened by derision, nor striking back in bitterness at those who mock it. The ypotryll is quite content, knowing it has its place in the world, even without praise or acclaim.

Just as the ypotryll is treated by small-minded people, so are all manner of creative ideas. The world may shower great praise upon a successful idea, but it is discouragingly critical of silly ideas, despite the crucial fact that one seldom imagines great things without imagining many silly things first. From the ypotryll therefore, we learn that the imagination must never fear to be ridiculous. A thousand absurd ideas are a necessary part of the process of populating the Realms of Imagination, so that, truly, silliness can be as valuable in its turn as the more practical ideas which it may help to inspire and evolve.

Of the ZHAHMATONIAN

The Zhahmatonians are all the various species inhabiting a most curious country called Zhahmat, of which three sorts are depicted here. The kuklopawn is a small, agile creature with a single eye. Because it does not possess binocular vision, it cannot accurately leap long distances, but moves in small vertical hops. It can deliver a vicious nip, but is primarily noted for its exceptional clarity of sight. The alfidi is a particular species of malacomorph with an olfactory sense to surpass that of the keenest bloodhound. It grazes upon moss and can move downhill easily by withdrawing into its shell and rolling. Travelling uphill is a longer, more laborious process, but as the country of Zhahmat is quite flat, the alfidi need not concern itself greatly. The quatrukhana is an amphibious creature which is rather ungainly on land, but propels itself quickly in water with its ring of nine webbed feet. Its four tentacles are extraordinarily sensitive and can not only detect and capture its insect prey, but are also equipped with stinging cells to subdue it.

The reader will readily note that each of these creatures apprehends the Zhahmatonian world in its own unique way, according to its own strengths: the kuklopawn with its vision, the alfidi with its sense of smell, and the quatrukhana with its tactile sensitivity. Each one is certainly accurate in its perception, and yet none can be sensible of all that there is to know. The Zhahmatonians thus remind us that each of us lays claim to some portion of the truth, but the whole truth is best discerned when we all contribute our own perceptions to enrich the understanding of the group, and accept, in turn, the perspectives imparted by others. Our best purpose is not individually to be correct, but rather to be open to the truth that is revealed when we seek it together.

Of the ZIZ

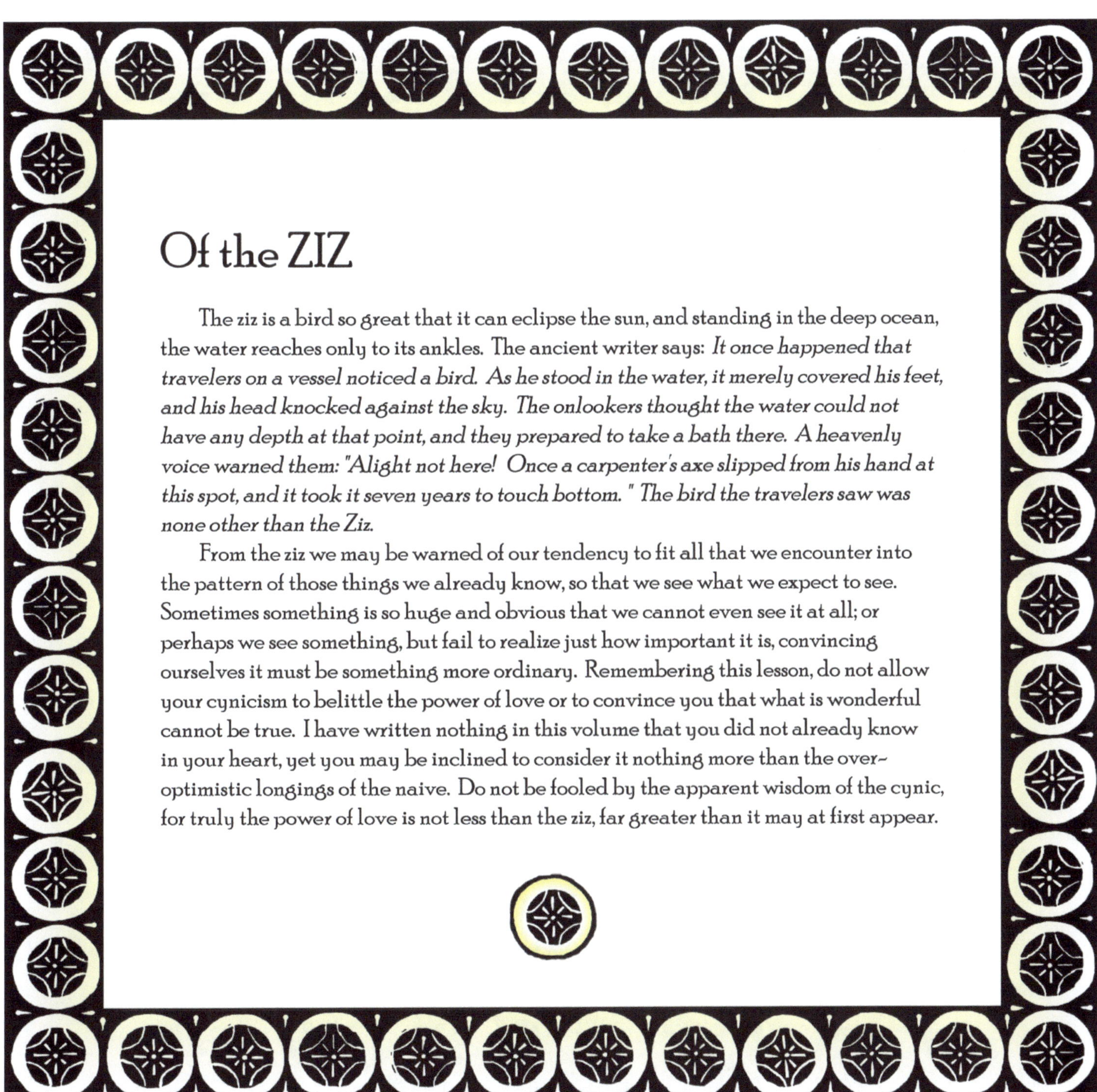

The ziz is a bird so great that it can eclipse the sun, and standing in the deep ocean, the water reaches only to its ankles. The ancient writer says: *It once happened that travelers on a vessel noticed a bird. As he stood in the water, it merely covered his feet, and his head knocked against the sky. The onlookers thought the water could not have any depth at that point, and they prepared to take a bath there. A heavenly voice warned them: "Alight not here! Once a carpenter's axe slipped from his hand at this spot, and it took it seven years to touch bottom." The bird the travelers saw was none other than the Ziz.*

From the ziz we may be warned of our tendency to fit all that we encounter into the pattern of those things we already know, so that we see what we expect to see. Sometimes something is so huge and obvious that we cannot even see it at all; or perhaps we see something, but fail to realize just how important it is, convincing ourselves it must be something more ordinary. Remembering this lesson, do not allow your cynicism to belittle the power of love or to convince you that what is wonderful cannot be true. I have written nothing in this volume that you did not already know in your heart, yet you may be inclined to consider it nothing more than the over-optimistic longings of the naive. Do not be fooled by the apparent wisdom of the cynic, for truly the power of love is not less than the ziz, far greater than it may at first appear.

821
POETRY
811
Poems
MILL
BOOKS
VOL I
VOL II
VOL III
GROCER
BAKER
MEATS
EV
XIV
Sauveylegs
THE 1001 NIGHTS
I
II
LIBRARY
Mandeville
Liure extra.
398
COLLECTED FAIRYTALES
S. MORGENSTERN
COMPLEAT HISTORY OF THE OTHER WORLD
398
398.1
Kircher
Topsell
MONSTRORVM HISTORIA
HISTORIÆ ANIMALIVM
Scamander
die Brüder Grimm
LANG
HISTORY OF THE FIVE KINGDOMS
History of the LANDS BEYOND
AEGN

# NOTES

Especially popular around the twelfth and thirteenth centuries, bestiaries were best-sellers of Medieval Europe, as well as North Africa and the Middle East. Bestiaries are, of course, collections of beasts, but the medieval ones that the word "bestiary" usually implies include not only natural history, but also all sorts of symbolism and moral lessons. Because it was a given that all of nature was made by the Creator to instruct and inspire humans, there was no separation between science books and allegorical works ~ it was all, equally, knowledge ~ and nor were the "facts" ever checked with the modern scientific method. Furthermore, bestiaries seldom involved original scholarship. Each one generally copied from previous texts including classical encyclopedias of natural history, travellers' tales of exotic marvels, and theological works. Thus bestiaries frequently include both real and fictional creatures, while the information about even the real animals includes all kinds of fantastical claims. This is half of what makes bestiaries so much fun.

The other half of the fun is the illustrations, sometimes whimsical, sometimes bizarre, sometimes beautiful, sometimes grotesque. The small paintings, and later wood block prints, depicting the array of creatures are often painstakingly done, but clearly owe more to imagination or convention than to direct observation. Their purpose was not accuracy, but inspiring wonder.

Bestiaries could vary widely in content and order, but their contents were not arranged alphabetically. Creatures were often grouped into land animals, birds, serpents, and sea creatures. The lion, as king of the beasts, was commonly featured first. I have arranged this bestiary as an alphabet book simply because abecedaries happen to be something I enjoy.

Bestiaries from the height of the genre's popularity were all hand written and illuminated, but with the invention of the printing press in the mid-fifteenth century, bestiaries and encyclopedias of natural history were among the early works to be printed and were unusually heavily illustrated. My illustrations are relief prints, although I have used rubber blocks in creating these images, rather than wood. Through the early centuries of printing, the labor and cost involved in carving original wood blocks made it very common for printers to reuse the same block multiple times within a book as well across multiple books. In this spirit, I have adapted some of the borders and additional illustrations in this book from blocks I originally carved for other projects.

This volume includes creatures from cultures all around the world because it is vitally important for us all to embrace and celebrate the full breadth of human imagination. The stories and images illustrating each creature are my own twists and interpretations of creatures that were, in most cases, first imagined by people other than myself. It is certainly never my intention to be inaccurate or disrespectful about the mythology of any people, but it is my intention to bring my own imagination to the party that has been going on all around the world as long as humans have been able to share their stories with one another.

In these notes I summarize some of the basic background of each creature, and I invite you to do further research on any that strike your fancy. There are many books and internet sites with information about fantastic and mythological creatures, and some are more reliable than others, of course. There is a distinct tendency for modern compilers of mythology, just like their medieval predecessors, to copy uncritically from previous sources, and indeed there may be instances in which I have fallen into the same trap. It is also worth noting that you will sometimes find contradictory information about creatures, which may be because of inaccuracy, but may also be because traditional stories do often encompass contradictions. I trust that your explorations in the Realms of Imagination will be undertaken in a spirit of wonder, appreciation, respect, and delight.

The first quotation in the introduction comes from the *Bestiary* of Philippe de Thaon from around 1125, as translated into modern English by Thomas Wright, 1841.

The second quotation comes from the *Book of Job* in the Hebrew Bible, probably from the sixth century BCE.

A

The **amphiptere** is a winged serpent, often with greenish-yellow feathers, bat-like wings, and an arrow-pointed tail tip. It comes from classical authors reporting tales of Egypt and Arabia, and it then developed into medieval European heraldry. The quotation in the text comes from the *History* of Herodotus, from about 440 BCE (English translation by George Rawlinson in 1858-60 with a touch of the translation by Henry Cary, 1876).

The **aspidochelone** comes from medieval European legend, although seafaring cultures around the world tell of island-like creatures of their own, including **pristis**, **Imap Umassoursa**, **Jasconius**, **Fastitocalon**, **Hafgufa** and **Lyngbakr**, **zaratan**, and **númhyalikyu**. The quotation in the text comes from the Old English *Physiologus* from the tenth century, as translated into modern English by Albert Stanburrough Cook in 1921.

B

The **baku** comes from Japanese folklore, where its dream-eating properties are first attested in the eighteenth century. The baku's appearance includes an elephant trunk and tiger paws, but it has changed over time to look more and more like a tapir. The quotation in the text comes from *Kottō, Being Japanese Curios, with Sundry Cobwebs*, by Lafcadio Hearn, from 1903.

Bonus! The **barnacle goose** is a botanical bird that grows on trees in a sort of seashell from which it hatches when ready to fly. It comes from medieval descriptions of Ireland. You can see a few in the picture of the author after these notes, although in the traditional accounts they grow from their beaks rather than their tails.

The **bunyip** is a fearsome water spirit or creature with a terrifying cry and a very wide variety of features. It has been variously described as being like an enormous starfish, having a head like a dog or crocodile, dark fur, horse tail, flippers, tusks or horns, and a duckbill. It comes from Australian Aboriginal mythology, with the added interpretations of European settlers in Australia. The quotation in the text comes from *The Geelong Advertiser*, 2 July 1845.

C

The **capybureau** is an invention, or perhaps a discovery, of my own.

The **cherufe** comes from the mythology of the Mapuche people of Chile. It is a monster from the magma pools within volcanoes and is the cause of volcanic eruptions and earth-quakes. It is sometimes said to be humanoid, sometimes more reptilian.

D

The **dragon** comes from medieval European legend, where it often serves as a symbol of evil. The first quotation in the text comes from *The Anglo-Saxon Chronicle* from the ninth century (modern English translation by James Henry Ingram, 1823). The second quotation comes from *The Faerie Queene* by Edmund Spenser, from 1590.

E

The **eale**, a sort of antelope with horns that can independently swivel 360°, was first described by Pliny the Elder in the first century CE, but became particularly well-known in Europe in the middle ages through the renaissance. There's some diversity in body type, from Pliny's description of a body like a hippopotamus to very slender, goat-like varieties. It is often spelled **yale**, and sometimes even **jall**. The quotation in the text comes from Solinus, from the third century, as translated in *The excellent and pleasant worke of Iulius Solinus Polyhistor* by Arthur Golding in 1587.

The **emela-ntouka** comes from the Congo in central Africa and is said to be the size of a small elephant with a long, heavy tail and a large, sharp horn on its nose. It eats plants.

F

The **fairy** comes from European mythology, particularly Celtic and the British Isles. The distinctions between elves, fairies, and other humanoid spirits are often rather confused, and the diminutive size and wings are a relatively recent addition to fairy lore, popularized in the nineteenth century. The quotation in the text comes from *The Muses Elizium* by Michael Drayton, from 1630.

The **fur-bearing trout** is in the family of Fearsome Critters, creatures of which tall tales were told by the lumberjacks and outdoorsmen of the United States frontier. Similar species have been attested in Canada and Iceland, and all these fish are said to grow their coat of thick fur because the waters where they live are so cold. Generally they have their origins as hoaxes and jokes.

G

The **gnome** is a small, ground-dwelling humanoid from folklore of northern Europe. The name was invented by Paracelsus in the sixteenth century to describe the elemental spirits of earth, but gnomes later absorbed characteristics of goblins, dwarves, and other "little people." They were originally considered to be guardians of underground treasures, and now are often guardians of gardens.

Bonus! The **grand marhoot** is a particularly gentle, thoughtful creature who loves to be surrounded by books. She is my own discovery, supported and inspired by Megan Christopher in honor of a beloved Friend. You can see one at the end of these notes.

The **griffin**, half lion, half eagle, comes from the legends of Greece, Egypt, the Middle East, Central Asia, and medieval Europe. The quotation in the text comes from *Pseudodoxia Epidemica* or *Vulgar Errors* by Thomas Browne in 1646, where in fact he was arguing that griffins do not exist.

H

The **hercinia** comes from European folklore and is a bird with feathers that shine with their own light so that it can guide travellers in the dark forest. The quotation in the text comes from *Love's Martyr* by Robert Chester, from 1601.

I

The **isnashi** comes from folklore of people in the Amazon rainforests of Brazil and Bolivia. There are varying descriptions of it, some saying it is more ape-like, others more sloth-like, some that it is carnivorous, others that it is vegetarian. It ~ or something similar ~ is also called the **mapinguari**.

J

Bonus! The **jinni** is a being from Arabian mythology, a sort of spirit that is neither angel nor demon, and is physical but often invisible. Magicians frequently attempt to summon and control jinn to take advantage of their powerful magical abilities. You can see one on the bookshelf in the frontispiece.

The **Jubjub bird** comes from the writings of Lewis Carroll. The quotations in the text come from *Jabberwocky* and *The Hunting of the Snark*, from 1871 and 1876.

K

The **kasa-obake** comes from Japanese folklore. It is usually depicted in the form of a closed umbrella with one leg, one eye, and a long tongue. Many people consider it to be a type of **tsukumogami**, a household object that becomes animate, usually after about 100 years. However, some reject this classification because there are no stories about the kasa-obake among the older legends of this type.

Bonus! The **kraken** is an enormous sea monster, originally described in ancient Scandinavian legend as having characteristics of a whale or crab. More recently it is generally understood to be a monstrous octopus or squid. You can see one in the picture of the **leviathan**.

L

The **leviathan** comes from Jewish legend, where it is the largest creature in the oceans, the counterpart of **behemoth**, the largest land creature, and **ziz**, the largest bird. The quotation in the text comes from the *Book of Job* probably from the sixth century BCE. (I have adapted and blended the wording from a number of different translations.)

The **lylit** is my own invention from the *Otherworld* series, and the story in the text comes from *Vision Revealed* from 2008. That tale was inspired by a folk tale from Patagonia. (The illustration is not from an actual block print, but was done digitally.)

M

The **malacomorph** is a modern word for the unnamed snail-shelled critters that appear with remarkable frequency among the illuminated borders of medieval manuscripts. They have nothing to do with the texts they adorn, which are usually Bibles, Books of Hours, and Psalters, and they seem to be whimsical bursts of imagination on the part of anonymous illuminators in medieval scriptoriums. The snail-bird is based on one that appears in the Luttrell Psalter from about 1325-40, while the others are my own whimsical bursts of imagination. There are a total of twelve malacomorphs throughout this bestiary.

The **mušḫuššu** is a dragonoid with feline forelegs, hind legs like an eagle, long neck and tail, and horns. It comes from ancient Mesopotamian mythology. It is also called a **sirrush**, although that name comes from a mistransliteration of the Sumerian. It is most famously depicted on the Ishtar Gate of Babylon, constructed in the sixth century BCE.

N

The **Ninki Nanka** comes from West African folklore, especially from Senegal and the Gambia, where it often plays the role of a "nursery bogey," a creature used to scare children into obedience. It is usually described as having a body like a crocodile, a neck like a giraffe, a head like a horse, and three horns.

O

The **ouroboros** is a snake biting its own tail to make a circle, and is a symbol of eternity rather than a creature about which there are actually any stories. It seems to have originated in ancient Egypt, and was enthusiastically adopted by medieval European alchemists.

P

The **phoenix** comes from ancient Greek and Roman descriptions of a bird that was said to be reborn at Heliopolis in Egypt. There is much variation in these descriptions, with the lifespan and the exact details of death and rebirth varying widely over time and between authors. The quotation in the text comes from a notebook of Leonardo da Vinci, from 1493–4, in the English translation by John Paul Richter, 1888.

The **pterippus** is the generic name for the winged horses of which Pegasus is the most famous individual. Indeed, Pegasus is the only one in classical Greek mythology. The quotation in the text comes from *Pegasus im Joche* by Friedrich von Schiller, from 1857 (English translation apparently by Moritz Retzsch, 1857).

Bonus! The **pyrallis** or **pyrausta** is a tiny four-legged, winged creature born of the fire of the copper-smelting furnaces of Cyprus. It cannot survive except in the fire. You can see two (although not with much detail) above the flames in the frontispiece, and another here.

Q

The **qilin** comes from Chinese mythology dating back to the fifth century BCE. They have hooves, antlers, and manes, and their bodies are scaled and sometimes flaming. They are peaceful vegetarians, who don't disturb the grass when they walk, and their voices sound like tinkling wind chimes. The quotation in the text comes from *The Shih Ching* or *Classic of Poetry* from the 8th to 7th century BCE, in the "metrical translation" by Clement Francis Romilly Allen, 1891.

R

The **robot** is of course not mythical, but in the world of science fiction and fantasy robots can be more than just machines capable of carrying out a complex series of actions automatically. They are artificially made and powered by clockwork or electronics, but once they're turned on, they can truly think for themselves with sentience, free will, and personalities of their own. This kind of robot originated in European science fiction. The word was coined by Josef Čapek in 1920. The quotation in the text comes from Tiktok, as reported in *Ozma of Oz* by L. Frank Baum from 1905. (I have combined sentences from several different speeches.)

S

The **salamander** comes from European folklore, adapted into alchemy by Paracelsus in the sixteenth century. The quotation in the text comes from a sermon entitled "Lessons From Nature" by C.H. Spurgeon, from 1871.

The **space creature** has been imagined in myriad forms by many cultures for the past four thousand years at least, as stories have been told of travellers to the heavens, the moon, and other planets. These particular creatures are my own. The quotation in the text comes from *Lumen* by Camille Flammarion, from 1872, in the English translation by A.A.M. and R.M., 1897.

Bonus! The **sea serpent** is a creature of many diverse types from many different cultures around the world. The most typical is a giant serpentine beast, usually with fins or flippers, which rears its long neck out of the water. You can see a sea serpent in the illustration on the front cover.

T

The **time fly** is my own discovery (although I suspect I'm not the only person ever to have thought of such an obvious pun). There is no "ancient writer" here except me.

The **troll** comes from Scandinavian folklore, where there are many variations, including the common report that trolls turn to stone when touched by sunlight, a variant which does not combine very well with the idea of a troll living under a bridge. The quotation in the text comes from *Norske Folkeeventyr* collected by P.C. Asbjørnsen in 1852, as translated by George Webbe Dasent in *Popular Tales from the Norse* (1858).

U

The **umbrellaphant** is an invention of various modern writers including Gustave Verbeek (1905) and Jack Prelutsky (2006). The quotation in the text comes from *The Terrors of the Tiny Tads* by Verbeek, who indeed portrays his umbrellaphant not as a welcoming creature, but as a "terror."

The **unicorn** comes originally from ancient Greek descriptions of India, but developed into its familiar form in the legends of medieval Europe. The single horn can both detect and prove an antidote to poison, and the unicorn itself is attracted to purity and innocence, which is why it can be captured by a virgin. The quotation in the text comes from a notebook of Leonardo da Vinci, from 1493-4, in the English translation by John Paul Richter, 1888.

 V

The **vegetable lamb** comes from European legend as early as the fifth century, and gained wide credence with the publication of the travel accounts of Friar Odoric (largely genuine, c. 1350) and Sir John Mandeville (largely fictitious, c. 1360). All these legends placed

the vegetable lambs in the general neighborhood of Tartary and Persia. The quotation in the text comes from Julius Caesar Scalager's *Exotericarum Exercitationum* from 1557, as translated in *Cathay and the Way Thither* by Sir Henry Yule, 1866.

 W

The **wyvern** comes from European folklore, although the distinction that wyverns have two legs while full dragons have four is strictly observed only in the heraldry of the British Isles. Wyverns are also generally smaller and weaker than the four-legged varieties of dragon, and usually cannot breathe fire or speak. The quotation in the text comes from *Wonder Tales of Ancient Wales* by Bernard Henderson and Stephen Jones, from about 1922.

The **wapaloosie** (*Geometrigradus cilioretractus*) is one of the Fearsome Critters of North American wilderness lore. The quotation in the text comes from *Fearsome Creatures of the Lumberwoods* by William T. Cox, from 1910.

X

The **xana** is a nymph or water spirit from the folklore of the Asturian region of northern Spain. In addition to luring men with their beauty and their song, they frequently guard treasures, which they may occasionally offer to worthy travellers. They are also known to leave their babies, called **xaninos**, with human women as changelings.

Y

The **yali**, also called **vyala**, comes from Indian mythology and began appearing in the architectural sculpture of southern India as early as the fourteenth century, where they are usually on pillars and cornices guarding temples. Types of yali have different styles of head including elephant, lion, bird, horse, and dog.

The **ypotryll** has the head of a boar complete with tusks, the body of a camel complete with humps, the legs of an ox or goat complete with hooves, and the tail of a serpent. It does not seem to exist outside of medieval European heraldry, and is rather rare even there.

Z

The **Zhahmatonians** are based on the shapes of chess pieces. Their landscape is a visual reference to John Tenniel's illustration of the chessboard country in *Through the Looking Glass* by Lewis Carroll, from 1871. I discovered these three creatures with the support and inspiration of the Paxson Helmreich family.

The **ziz** is a bird so huge that its wingspan can block out the sun. It is the avian counterpart of **leviathan** and **behemoth** from Jewish mythology. Some sources describe it as being like a **griffin**, while others say it's like a giant rooster. I like to think that its legs are enormously long, like a heron, the better to wade in the ocean. The quotation in the text comes from *The Legends of the Jews* by Louis Ginzberg, from 1913.

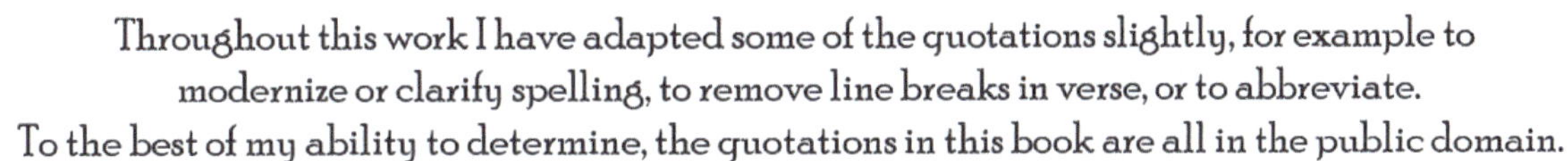

Throughout this work I have adapted some of the quotations slightly, for example to
modernize or clarify spelling, to remove line breaks in verse, or to abbreviate.
To the best of my ability to determine, the quotations in this book are all in the public domain.

There may be cases where I have been unable to trace a copyright holder; if so
I will be happy to correct any omissions upon notification.

From the GRAND MARHOOT we learn
that gentleness and laughter bring light wherever they rest.

Of the AUTHOR

If it should seem presumptuous to undertake so lofty a study as the mythical creatures of cultures all around the Earth and through history, let my defense be the great love and respect I bear for the works of the Imagination in all places and by all peoples. In hope that I may be deemed not too unworthy a writer on this noble topic, I plead my extensive travel in these Fantastic Realms. I cannot say when I first discovered my love of magical beasts, but by the age of six I was deeply immersed in the Kingdoms of **Fairy**, and at seven my favorite books included those of the most commendable author and illustrator Bill Peet, who treated of fantastical creatures including the **dragon**, the **sea serpent**, the **whingdingdilly**, and the **wump**. At the age of nine and ten I was insatiable in the reading of fairy tales of the world, particularly those collected by the inestimable Andrew Lang. I was soon exploring new lands of my own discovery, and observing such creatures as the **vinket**, the **pinkle**, and the **gublip**. By my high school years I was recording the histories and natures of a world that was eventually to become the basis of my *Otherworld* series. When I attended college at **Yale** University I received a degree in linguistics, studying at a campus generously endowed with mythical creatures adorning the architecture, including the very **griffin** pictured in this work. I then taught middle school art for ten years, where flights of imagination were a constant presence in the classroom, and I am now working from home as a writer and artist while raising two children of the next generation of travellers in the Realms of Imagination.

I display my art and books in numerous shows, and in 2019 I was greatly honored to be awarded The Directors' Choice Art Show Award at the Arisia Convention for the series of mythical animals presented in this volume. The body of work including many of these creatures was also awarded an Art Show Judge's Choice Award at the Boskone 56 Convention in the same year. It is with such encouragement as this that I make bold to present this bestiary, in the hope that it may inspire the Esteemed Reader to further contemplation on the use of the Imagination in bettering our world.

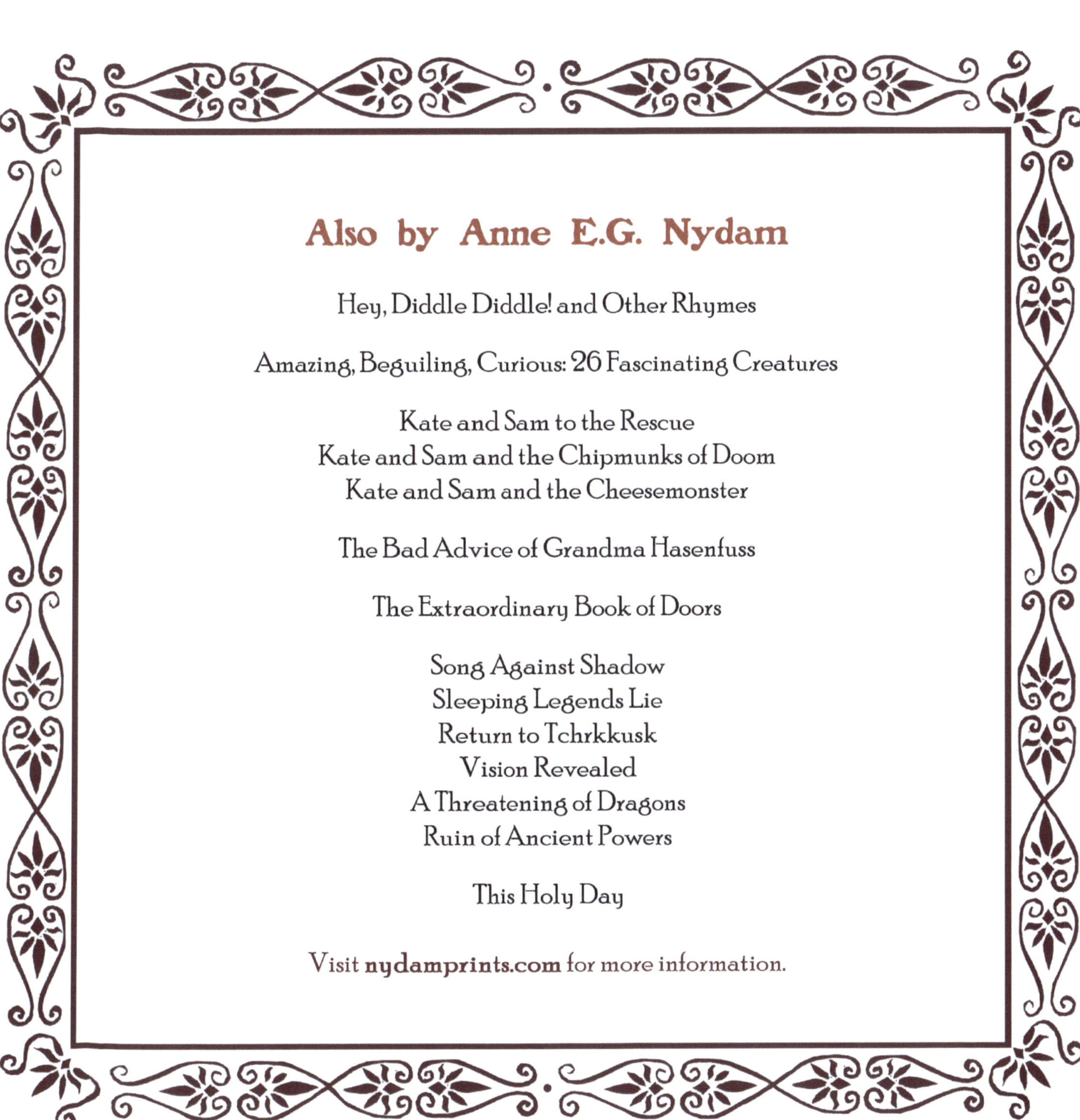

Also by Anne E.G. Nydam

Hey, Diddle Diddle! and Other Rhymes

Amazing, Beguiling, Curious: 26 Fascinating Creatures

Kate and Sam to the Rescue
Kate and Sam and the Chipmunks of Doom
Kate and Sam and the Cheesemonster

The Bad Advice of Grandma Hasenfuss

The Extraordinary Book of Doors

Song Against Shadow
Sleeping Legends Lie
Return to Tchrkkusk
Vision Revealed
A Threatening of Dragons
Ruin of Ancient Powers

This Holy Day

Visit **nydamprints.com** for more information.